MW01027240

RETRIEVER RANSOM

PET WHISPERER P.I.

MOLLY FITZ

Editor: Jennifer Lopez (No, seriously!)

Cover & Graphics Designer: Cover Affairs

Proofreader: Jasmine Jordan

This is a work of fiction. Names, characters, organizations, places, events, and incidents are either products of the author's imagination or are used fictitiously. Any resemblance to actual persons, living or dead, or actual events is purely coincidental.

Whiskered Mysteries
https://whiskeredmysteries.com/

ABOUT THIS BOOK

A new year means a new mayor in the sleepy seaside town of Glendale. Unfortunately, not everyone's happy about his election. In fact, someone's so unhappy that they kidnap his beloved golden retriever and leave a ransom note claiming they'll only return the dog when the man resigns his position.

Enter Angie and Octo-Cat with their first official paying case. Little does the mayor know that while they work to safely recover his ransomed retriever, they'll also be investigating his past to figure out why someone would go so far to keep him out of office.

Can a talking cat find a missing dog? Will he

even want to? Find out in the latest adventure of Pet Whisperer P.I.

To anyone who wishes she could talk to her animal best friend...
Well, what's stopping you?

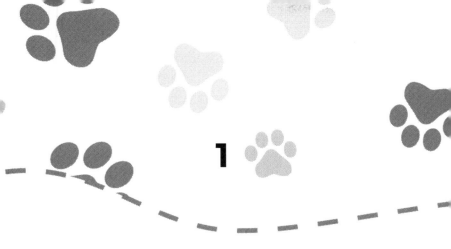

My name is Angie Russo. I live in the Blueberry Bay region of Maine, and I can talk to animals. Thanks to this unique—but mostly secret—skill, I've taken to solving mysteries around town.

Usually my involvement happens because I have a tendency to wind up in the wrong place at the wrong time, but now I've also hung out my hat as a private investigator. And just because I don't have any clients, that doesn't mean I'm not good at what I do.

Or more accurately, that we're not good at what we do.

Yeah, my cat is my business partner, and we also get help from my quirky nan, her sweet Chihuahua

Paisley, my lawyer boyfriend Charles, and even the handful of animals that live near our property—most notably, Pringle the raccoon who lives in a luxury tree fort in our backyard and is a tad addicted to reality TV.

Nan and Charles can't talk to the animals like I do.

In fact, I've never met another living soul who can, and I still don't know why I was blessed with this particular ability. All I know is that I got zapped by a faulty coffee maker, knocked unconscious, and woke up with a talking cat on my chest.

At first, I could only understand that one cat, but over time, my powers grew stronger. Now I can understand most animals, but occasionally I do still find a dud.

That same crabby tabby, Octo-Cat, wound up with me after we worked together to solve the murder of his previous owner. He came with a generous trust fund, a large coastal manor, and an endless string of color commentary about my life.

He has a girlfriend, a former show Himalayan named Grizabella. Their relationship is long distance and mostly sustained through my Instagram account. It's equal parts adorable, hilarious, and groan-inducing.

But, hey, a happy cat means a happy me.

And I have a lot to be happy about lately, especially since my bad luck often results in good outcomes. First there was the zap that gave me Octo-Cat, then Nan's impulsiveness landed Paisley in our lives, but those are nothing compared to the fact that a huge family secret had recently been cracked wide open.

Mom and I found out that Nan hadn't been completely honest about our family's origins even though she'd had more than fifty years to come clean. And, well, as awful as that whole thing was to discover, it also meant we were able to connect with long-lost family in Georgia, and thus I found the sister I never had in my cousin Mags.

She came for a visit over the holidays and that went well...

Mostly.

She still doesn't know my secret, but I think I'll tell her next time we're together. I probably should have told her before she returned home, but I was scared it would make her and the rest of our newfound family reject me.

I mean, did you believe me at first when I said I could talk to animals?

It's totally crazy, but also totally true and totally

a defining feature of my life—and I wouldn't have it any other way.

That brings us to today.

We just celebrated the start of a new year. Normally I don't make resolutions, but this time I decided to do whatever it takes to finally get Octo-Cat's and my P.I. business off the ground. Even though we can easily live off his trust fund and Nan's retirement, there's a special brand of shame in having to be supported by your cat.

I mean, I have seven associate degrees.

At least one of those should be good for a job.

And a job is exactly what I'll have to get if my business doesn't take off this year. My boyfriend Charles said he'd welcome me back at the law firm anytime, and while I love him dearly, I always hated being a paralegal.

It doesn't matter, though, because I will succeed at this P.I. thing.

I'm too stubborn not to.

Besides, I'd really hate to let down my cat...

* * *

"This is so exciting," Nan trilled as we stood outside of city hall with a small crowd of other Glendalians to watch the incoming mayor get sworn into office.

Paisley barked merrily from within my grandmother's arms.

Octo-Cat had requested to stay home, given his disdain for crowds, and that was a battle I hadn't wanted to fight.

The mayor appeared at the top of the steps dressed in a fine navy suit with a light blue dress shirt and matching tie. At forty-seven, he was at least two decades younger than his predecessor. But while Mayor McHenry had been a family man, incoming mayor Dennison was a proud bachelor.

When asked about his singlehood by the press, he always said that his trusty golden retriever was more than enough family for him. Besides, less of a home life made it easier for him to give his full attention to making the humble town of Glendale the best it could be. Good answer, right?

As Dennison moved toward the podium now, a harsh boo rose from the crowd. Nan and I spun and saw a line of protestors holding signs that called for the new mayor to be ousted before he'd even fully taken up office.

"That's in poor taste," Nan hissed, shaking her head.

"Why does everyone hate him so much?" I whispered.

She shrugged. "Any time the party in office changes, somebody's bound to be unhappy about it. The whole country's a powder keg, so why not our town, too?"

I returned my gaze to Dennison, who stood stock-still with an unreadable expression. Poor guy. He'd won the election fair and square, yet he couldn't even enjoy this pinnacle moment in his career.

"What's going on, Mommy?" Paisley asked, wagging her tail in excitement, misreading the mood of the crowd.

I kissed her on the head and whispered, "Don't worry about it."

As much as I loved the optimistic little dog, explaining everything to her all the time often became exhausting—especially when we were in public and I couldn't speak freely.

"People of Glendale," the new mayor's voice boomed despite the continuing sounds of protest.

"Thank you for electing me to serve as your mayor."

The boos and calls for him to resign grew louder.

Nan whooped and cheered beside me even though I knew for a fact she hadn't voted for him. She smiled at me sheepishly. "Poor guy. Someone needs to encourage him."

Now we both cheered.

Dennison's eyes met mine, and he nodded subtly before continuing. "I promise to do everything in my power to make these next four years prosperous and safe for all of us. Thank you."

He dipped his head, then disappeared back inside the building.

Octo-Cat would definitely be upset at having missed the drama of this day.

"Well, that was the shortest inauguration I've ever seen, and I've been to all of them since moving out here some forty years ago," Nan mused.

"I'm sure it will be fine," I mumbled. "People just need time to cool off after the election."

"Yes, because all of November and December and most of January obviously weren't enough," Nan responded after sucking air through her teeth.

We stood in place waiting for the crowd to

disperse. Some of them did, but the protestors seemed to grow in number as they crept closer to the stairs outside city hall.

"Let's get out of here," Nan said, shaking her head sadly.

I couldn't agree more.

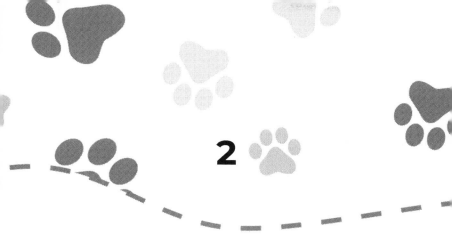

2

I sat in the enormous bay window of my home library sipping an oversized mug of English breakfast tea while watching the snow swirl past.

Octo-Cat sat at my feet flicking his tail back and forth to the tuneless hum of our mostly silent house. "You wouldn't catch me dead in that mess."

I lowered my mug and cuddled deeper into the woven afghan wrapped around my shoulders. "What? The snow?"

He scoffed at my apparent naivete. "Snow, yeah. You can't fool me. It's nothing but semi-solid water. No, thank you."

"You know..." A smile crept across my face as I waited for him to turn toward me. "Maine Coons supposedly love water, and you are part Maine Coon, right?"

He always claimed to be, but we both knew that was a lie.

Octo-Cat's eyes slitted and his tail stilled. "Yes," he answered slowly, cautiously. "But I'm also part tabby. Tabbies don't like the water."

"Of course." I took another sip of tea to prevent a chuckle from escaping. Far be it from me to point out that Tabby was a coloration and not a breed. Everything Octavius said had to be taken at face value, lest we upset him.

He'd also gone to the Holiday Spectacular last month when the ground was covered in fresh snowfall and hadn't complained too much —at least not for him. It seemed we'd now crossed the acceptable level of snow since then. Either that or he was passing judgment on my less than stellar job keeping up with the shoveling.

Light clacking sounded on the floorboards, and a moment later Paisley appeared, tail wagging in its usual dark blur. "Hello, Mommy. Can I cuddle, too?"

Octo-Cat groaned and rolled his eyes when the Chihuahua jumped onto my lap.

"I wanted to say hi before Nan and I go on our run. Hi!"

I gaped down at her. "You're running in this?" The snow had to be twice as deep as she was tall.

She blinked wide eyes at me, confused by this question. "Why, yes. We run every day, come heck or high water."

"Water," Octo-Cat emphasized with a pointed flick of his tail. "Told you it was water."

Nan and Paisley had started their recreational running hobby on January first and had kept up with it every day since. That was my grandmother for you. She always had a number of hobbies going, usually at least one that was artistic and one fitness based. Often many more than that, too.

This month's commitment to running, however, seemed to be more about me than about herself. I often pointed out the fact my seventy-something Nan was in far better shape than twenty-something me, and that had become incredibly evident last month when we ran around downtown Glendale chasing killers, kidnappers, and more.

Apparently, I'd complained a bit too loudly and too often, because now Nan invited me to join her every single day—and I said "no" every single day.

Did she really think I'd be up for starting a new

exercise regimen at the height of the cold season? Nope. No, thank you.

Sure enough, my worst fears were answered when Nan appeared about five minutes later. She was wearing a hot pink velour tracksuit and held a leopard print coat with a fur collar draped over one arm. "C'mon, we've got to get going a little early today. I have a quick stop-off to make before we hit the trail."

I doubted there was a trail, unless she'd woken up early to shovel one herself. A giant yawn pushed its way out from my chest as a massive shiver racked through my body. "You and Paisley have fun out there!"

"Oh, no. Today you're coming too," Nan insisted, reaching for my hand and attempting to pull me from my seat.

I ripped away as if she'd scalded me with her soft touch. "Ha, ha. Nice try. Today's answer is the same as it's been every other day you've asked me. Octo-Cat and I will hold down the fort here. See you when you're back."

"Nope. I'm not taking no for an answer this time." She crossed her arms over her chest and narrowed her gaze threateningly.

"Why not? You've taken it every other day." I was pushing my luck and I knew it.

She motioned toward the galactic space cats calendar that hung on the wall above my desk, then groaned and marched over to it. Flipping the page up, she pointed to a calico kitten flying through the stars in a giant cartoon taco shell. "It's the first day of a new month. February."

I stayed silent, accepting that the more I argued the harder she'd come down on me in the end.

Nan, however, refused to be dismissed. "You may have completely flubbed up January, but a new month means a new start."

"Can I maybe start in a warmer month?" I glanced out the window again. Everything was white—the ground, the sky, my reflection as all the color drained from my face in fear. She meant it this time.

I was doomed, but I still had to give my resistance one last ill-fated shot. "I don't have anything to run in," I complained and forced a sad look.

"Ahh, but you do." A giant smile lit Nan's face. "You'll find a new jogging suit that matches mine exactly. I also picked up some sport boots and thick wool socks. Everything's waiting for you in your room. Chop, chop. Like I said, we have a quick stop-off to make before hitting the trail."

Not even cute corn shell taco cats in outer space could save me now. I lifted my eyes to meet her, telepathically pleading for her to have some mercy.

It did not work.

"Five minutes," she said firmly and then began tapping her foot, already beyond the limits of her patience with me. "Then I'm dragging you outside, whether or not you're ready."

We both knew she'd push me butt naked into the snow if I took even a second longer. We also both knew that she was the stronger of the two of us.

I raced out of the library and up to my tower bedroom to get ready. Octo-Cat's smug laughter followed me every step of the way.

3

gripped the handle for the passenger side door of Nan's little red sports coupe, but it didn't budge. Normally, Nan not only unlocked the car in advance but she also remote started it so the interior would be toasty warm by the time we took off.

"We're taking your car," she called from the porch as she locked up then descended with Paisley in tow.

My car, however, was not where I usually parked it.

Noting my hesitation, Nan pointed toward the far side of the house.

My breaths burst out in icy puffs. As much as I

didn't look forward to running, at least it would make me warm. Right?

The moment I spotted my car, an indignant groan ripped right through me. My once-modest sedan had been outfitted with a hot pink snowplow. "What's this?" I screamed.

Nan passed by me, opened the door, and situated herself in the driver's seat. "For making the trail, of course."

Oh, of course. "Why is it hot pink?"

She shot me a proud grin. "Because that's my favorite color. You know that. I had it custom made."

"And did you put it on all by yourself, too?" I managed. Even though my grandmother was in fantastic shape, it was hard imagining her heaving this enormous thing around single-handedly.

She waved off my question with a deft swirl of her hand. "Don't be silly. I called Cal over to help."

Great. The next time I saw our favorite local handyman, he'd be getting a very stern talking to. I climbed into the passenger seat and buckled up.

Paisley immediately put her paws on the door and stared out the ice-covered window. I couldn't imagine she saw much.

"Why are we in the car? We don't need the car for running. We use our feet!"

Personally, I had other questions in mind. "Are you sure my car can handle this? There's a reason these things are usually on trucks."

Nan snorted. "This one's made of plastic instead of metal. I'm sure we'll be fine."

Uh-huh. Famous last words.

Besides, how else are we supposed to carve out our running trail?" She turned the key in the ignition and my tacky, made-over car sputtered to life. We jerked forward, then stopped again just as suddenly.

"What happened?" I demanded of my grandmother.

She ignored me and pushed down on the gas pedal again. Nothing happened this time.

"Huh. Well, it was working last night" was the only thing she said about that.

"Too bad. I guess no running for us today." I was already halfway out of the car and looking forward to a second cup of steaming hot tea in my favorite reading spot when Nan popped out of the car and called me to a stop.

"Not so fast," she called after me. "We'll take my car."

I kept going, so close to being free to return to my regularly scheduled day. "If my car can't handle that plow, there's no way yours can."

"Paisley, I'm sorry, but you'll have to stay here. The snow's too deep," Nan explained, returning to the porch and setting the Chihuahua down beside the electronic pet door.

The poor little dog whined and looked to me for help. "Mommy, tell Nan I want to come. I always come."

I didn't need to translate that. Paisley's whimpering and low-hung tail said it all. "I wish it was you instead of me, but Nan's right about the snow being too deep."

"Nonsense," Paisley cried, then bolted down the stairs and took a flying leap into the nearest snowdrift, disappearing immediately. Not even the tips of her giant foxlike ears showed above the bank.

I rushed forward and scooped her into my arms.

She was too shocked to do anything other than shiver. "Cold. C-c-c-cold!"

"We'll be back soon," I promised loudly, then whispered just to Paisley, "Seriously. As soon as possible."

She cried again as I set her back beside the pet door.

"Why don't you go see what Octo-Cat is doing and if you can help?" I suggested.

And just like that, her tail lifted and began to wag once more. She pushed through the pet door, barking happily and calling for our cat housemate.

"All good?" Nan asked, quirking a questioning eyebrow my way.

"With Paisley at least," I grumbled but followed her back toward the sports coupe and dutifully sank inside. This was going to be nothing short of torture.

"Where are we going?" I asked a few moments later when she still hadn't explained herself.

"A friend from my community art class needs some extra help. This weather really triggers the arthritis in her joints, and with her twin grandkids off at college this year, she has no one to walk Cujo."

I gasped in horror. "Cujo? I know we live in Stephen King's home state, but c'mon. What kind of name is that for a dog, given, well, everything Cujo did?"

Nan sighed but didn't turn to face me. "Big talk from someone who named her pet Octo-Cat."

I wanted to laugh but luckily held it together. "Please tell me he's not a Saint Bernard."

"No, he's a mutt. Husky mixed with something else. They're not sure what."

Well, we would find out soon enough.

And sure enough, even with the deep snow and icy roads, we were at Nan's friend's house five short minutes later.

"Wait here," she instructed, marching around to the back of the house and returning with an enormous fuzzy beast on lead a few minutes later.

She motioned for me to get out and join them. "Might as well start our run from here."

"Is that Cujo?" I asked, eyeing the dog hesitantly. He may not have been a Saint Bernard, but he was almost as big as one. His light blue—almost white—eyes made him even more unnerving to look at.

Nan chuckled. "Who else would it be, dear?"

"Stop looking at me like that," the dog said, reminding me that—oh, yeah—I could talk to animals.

"Like what?" I asked, voice shaking with equal parts cold and nervousness.

"A human who talks? Curious." Cujo breezed right past this revelation and answered my question head-on.

"Stop looking at me the way everyone does. Like

I'm going to eat you. If the way you smell is any indication, you'd taste terrible."

He opened his mouth and panted in what I assumed was a self-aggrandizing laugh. "Look, I'm a working dog. That means I focus on the job that needs to be done, and right now, that's assisting your grandmother on her run."

"Fair enough," I answered, forcing myself to look away from his steely gaze.

"Hike! Hike!" Nan shouted and then took off at a pace I doubted I'd be able to match.

"Wait for me," I cried as she and the oversized husky tore through the snow-covered suburban street.

The day had just begun, and already I was more than ready to get it over with.

4

'm pretty sure I almost died that morning.

Only almost, though.

Thankfully I managed to complete that wretched run without falling face forward into the snow like I feared every time my boot landed wrong on the poorly plowed street.

As much as I wanted to get in better shape, I didn't think sprinting through a snowstorm was the way to do it. Cujo, however, seemed to heartily disagree. During the entire half-hour ordeal, he barked encouragements to both me and Nan, acting as our own personal doggie drill sergeant.

"Pick up the pace! That's it! Let's go! Hike!" he shouted while tugging hard on the leash and

forcing us all to move as fast as our feet could carry us.

When we finally returned to his yard, he gave me a long piteous look and laid his ears back flat against his head. "You didn't do a very good job today. We'll have to train much harder so that you're ready."

"Ready for what?" I barked back, already beginning to shiver now that we'd stopped moving.

"Whatever comes next," he answered—whether cryptically or dismissively I couldn't quite tell. I also didn't quite care, given my current level of exhaustion.

"Now that wasn't so bad, was it?" Nan asked once we'd both settled back into her car. She couldn't fool me, though. Even she had a hard time catching her breath after that muttsky-driven workout.

I laughed and leaned my head against the seat rest. Everything burned. Everything hurt. And I already knew Nan would force me to do the whole thing all over again tomorrow... and the next day... and the next day.

Working out with Nan would easily prove to be worse than a prison sentence. I just hoped warden Cujo's time with us would be brief. I much preferred Paisley's personal brand of encouragement—and her pace, too.

"Good effort out there today, dear. You've earned your sweets," Nan told me when we arrived back home. Still brimming with energy, she scuttled into the kitchen to pick up with some mid-morning baking.

I could have argued the senselessness of exercising when we would only use it as an excuse to pile back on double or triple the calories in desserts but knew that somehow pointing this out would only lead to longer and more intense workouts. No thank you!

I had just begun the now painful climb up the stairs to my library when the doorbell chimed overhead.

Ping. Ping. Ding bing, it sounded to the tune of "Eye of the Tiger," proving once and for all that Nan had planned today's forced fitness well in advance.

"Coming!" I yelled and then slowly turned myself around. Ouch, ouch, ouch.

"What happened to you?" Octo-Cat asked while effortlessly trotting down the stairs and thus throwing his ease of mobility right in my poor, tired face.

"Nan happened to me," I grumbled after drawing in a deep, ragged breath.

He raised a paw and chuckled. "Say no more."

The doorbell chimed again.

Octo-Cat's eyes glowed hot with judgment. "Well, aren't you going to get that?"

"Coming!" I shouted again and forced myself to hobble faster through the foyer.

When I flung the door open with a giant grin of relief, I found a familiar face staring right back at me from the porch. "Mayor D-D-Dennison," I sputtered in surprise. "To what do we owe the pleasure?"

Octo-Cat plopped himself down beside me, willing to brave the cold tendrils of air reaching in through the open doorway so that he could gain a front-row seat to whatever happened next.

The mayor removed his hat—an oversized Russian shapka—to reveal a messy head of hair. "May I please come in?"

"Angie!" Nan called as she hurried toward us, her gait completely unmired from that morning's workout whereas I could hardly walk. "Is that the mayor? Well, don't leave him standing out in the cold!"

She pushed past me and wrapped a motherly

arm around Mayor Dennison's broad shoulders to usher him toward the living room. "Let's have a hot cup of tea to warm you up, then you can tell us everything."

"Nan," I interrupted. "He still hasn't told us why he's here."

"Perfect, then he can tell us over tea. Gossip always goes down easiest with a nice, steaming mug in your hands. Wouldn't you say?" Without waiting for either of us to respond, she returned to the kitchen, leaving me to make awkward small talk with the mayor at least half the town of Glendale never wanted.

"Got a lot of snow out there," I mumbled like an idiot. It was February in Blueberry Bay. Of course there was snow.

He nodded, smiled, glanced toward the kitchen.

I didn't want to ask about politics since I already knew there was some contention there, but I also knew better than to ask about the purpose of his visit before Nan returned with the tea.

Luckily, Paisley came frolicking to our rescue, hopping right up onto the mayor's lap. "I smell a doggie!" she trilled, wagging her tail curiously.

"She likes you," I said with a grin. "Are you a dog person?"

Octo-Cat hissed somewhere from the other side of the room. He didn't even like that question to be asked, let alone answered.

"I have—well, had—a dog," the mayor answered with a wistful sigh. "Actually, that's why I'm here. I—"

"Oh no, you don't!" Nan hurried back into the living room, balancing a small serving tray with three cups of tea and all the fixings. "Not without me."

Our visitor cleared his throat and folded his hands in his lap while Nan served. When at last we were all seated comfortably with our beverages and snacks, my grandmother motioned for him to continue. "Now you may continue."

"I came because I heard you're a private investigator," he said to Nan, completely ignoring the mug that she'd handed to him.

She chortled at this. "Not me. Her."

She pointed at me, and I waved awkwardly.

"Okay, either way. I need to hire you to help me." He glanced pointedly in my direction.

"What seems to be the problem?" I asked, feeling oh so professional in that moment. Here I was, a proper investigator being called in to help the man who held the top political official in all of

Glendale. It didn't get any bigger than this for a small-town P.I.

But then he spoke again and shattered my newfound delusions of grandeur. "My dog, actually. He's gone missing."

I choked on my tea, which led to an awkward coughing fit. "Your dog?" I asked hoarsely. "What? Did he run away?"

"No," he said firmly. "Marco didn't leave on his own. He was taken."

Nan raised a delicate eyebrow. "What makes you so sure?"

"Because the kidnapper left a note. A ransom note." After delivering this news, the mayor finally took a sip of his tea, much to Nan's satisfaction.

I sat back against the couch. My body remained tired, but my mind zoomed to life, a million gears all clicking at once.

Maybe this could still be a fascinating case, after all.

5

"I brought it with me," Mayor Dennison explained, then withdrew the folded ransom note from his wallet. He handed it over to me, and Nan edged closer to read it over my shoulder, her lips moving as she soundlessly voiced each word.

The note was typed on a plain white piece of computer paper. The font was so large it filled the entire page with just a few harsh words: Resign. Or the dog gets it.

"Well, what do they mean by that?" Nan quipped. "They should have been more specific."

For the first time, I noticed that the usually stoic mayor had tears in his eyes. "Do you really think they'd hurt Marco?" he asked, momentarily casting his gaze toward the floor.

I swallowed down the dry lump in my throat and said, "I don't know," rather unhelpfully. We still had no idea who they could be.

"Please find out who did this," he begged, actually folding his hands and shaking them my way. "I'll pay. I'll pay whatever you need. Marco is the only family I have. We've been through it all together, and I can't stand the thought of anything untoward happening to him."

"Who would want you to resign so badly that they'd resort to dognapping?" I asked, forcing myself to remain focused on the facts.

At the same time, Nan blurted out, "Of course we'll take your case. Consider us hired."

He glanced back and forth between us, apparently unsure who he should address first.

Octo-Cat appeared from wherever he'd been hiding and jumped onto the coffee table right beside Nan's carefully arranged tea service. As he flicked his tail, he stared down his nose at the mayor, appraising our new client. "I don't know if I want to help find a lost dog," he said with a sneer. "This will forever go down in history as our first paying case, and it's about a stupid dog?"

Paisley whined and covered her snout with her paws.

But Octo-Cat continued unperturbed. "I mean, it's not even dead. We've been on a roll with the murders lately. Last time, we helped solve two murders. Two! Don't you see? A dognapping case is beneath us."

I shot my cat a disgusted look, wishing I could give him a firm tongue-lashing. Unfortunately, I had to ignore his sandpaper barbs as the mayor sat eyeing me intently.

"Yes, we'll take the case. In fact, it will be our top priority," I said with what I hoped was a reassuring nod.

"Yeah," Octo-Cat drolled. "Because we don't have any other cases right now."

I swept my hand across the coffee table and knocked him to the floor. "Bad kitty," I said emphatically, knowing I'd pay for it later.

"Do you have any pictures of Marco?" Nan asked before taking a long slurp of her quickly cooling tea.

"He's a golden retriever. Looks like a standard golden retriever, no unique markings or anything. I post all kinds of photos on my Facebook page, though, if you need them."

"Thank you. That would be helpful," I said, taking back over. I was the P.I. here, after all. "What we really need to talk about, though, is your enemies."

"My enemies?" he asked, taken aback. His jaw set in a firm, hard line, and his eyes turned colder than our tea.

"Clearly you have some if one of them would resort to ransoming Marco. But before we get into that, would it be okay for me to address you by your first name or do you prefer it to be more formal...?"

He shook his head, his normally placid expression returning just as quickly as it had left. "Yes, of course. Call me Mark."

It struck me then that I either hadn't heard his first name before or that I'd at least never connected the fact that he'd named his dog after himself, then tacked on one extra syllable. Mark. Marco.

"Mark," I said, forcing myself to keep a straight face. "Mark it is."

We all sat silently for a moment.

"Now, I know it can't be easy to talk about, but it's important. Given the show at the inauguration, your election has been quite controversial. Why is that?"

Although I didn't follow politics closely, I'd read

the odd news report on this topic. Still, I wanted to get Mark's take on the situation to see what added insights he could provide.

He licked his lips and steepled his fingers before him. "The usual things mostly. The fact I'm a bachelor is a big one. How can a single man be committed to building a family community? they all ask." He scoffed at this, pausing briefly before he continued.

"And as you know, the vote was quite close. I won by hardly more than a percentage point. My opponent's supporters demanded a recount, but that was ultimately deemed a waste of taxpayers' money, and so I was sworn in."

I knew all this. The mayor had to be holding something back. Neither of these reasons were enough for someone to threaten harm to a lovable golden retriever, whether or not they disliked his owner. Golden retrievers were largely considered America's top family dog, and I'm sure it won back some points for the mayor that he had one.

Still, something wasn't quite adding up.

"Is that all?" I asked cautiously.

"That's all," Mark assured me with a quick nod.

Octo-Cat settled himself onto my feet, but not before giving my big toe a solid bite as punishment for my stunt earlier. "He's lying," the tabby informed me with a low growl.

I took a deep steadying breath, then focused my gaze back on the mayor. "Are you sure there's nothing else? No other possible reason for the kidnapping?"

"None," Mark insisted, smiling reassuringly in my direction.

"He's still lying," Octo-Cat revealed, but I could now see that for myself, too. "Definitely lying."

"Oh...kay," I said slowly, breaking the small word into two distinct sounds. "Then why don't you tell me about the last few days. Did anything unusual happen? Did anyone seem extra interested in Marco at this time?"

As I listened to the mayor prattle on about his busy life, I couldn't help wondering why he'd hire me and then withhold at least part of the truth.

A dishonest client, no doubt, would make solving the case much more difficult. Still, I couldn't allow Marco to suffer for his owner's crimes—whatever they were.

I guess we'd be finding out soon enough.

6

fter Mayor Dennison left, Nan, the animals, and I huddled together at the large dining room table to recap.

"So we have another kidnapping," Nan said thoughtfully. "We've dealt with those before. Recently at that."

She was right. I'd already been thinking about our past abduction cases myself. They had both proven to be the most nerve-wracking investigations I'd ever faced. Both had hit incredibly close to home, too.

First, Octo-Cat disappeared at the exact same time the other beneficiaries of Ethel Fulton's will had called for an arbitration in an attempt to relieve him of his inheritance. The culprit in that case had been exceedingly angry when we'd found Octo-Cat and taken him back—she'd even wound up with a nasty cat-inflicted wound that would probably scar. We'd seen neither hide nor hair of the folks involved in that kidnapping in the time since.

Then the second one happened. On Christmas Eve, my cousin Mags had been taken right off the street at the annual Holiday Spectacular fair. She'd been kept blindfolded and was ultimately let go when the crooks—a man and a woman—got spooked and ran.

They'd meant to take me but had mistakenly abducted my eerily similar looking cousin instead. They called her "Russo"—my last name—and warned her to keep her nose out of places where it didn't belong.

Well, Mags had returned to her home in Larkhaven, Georgia, no worse for the wear, and we hadn't heard from her mysterious kidnappers since.

I doubted the ransomed retriever had anything to do with either of those cases, but reviewing our history at least gave us a place to start with this new investigation.

"Are you thinking about when Mags and Octo-Cat were taken?" Nan asked, steepling her fingers and tapping them against her chin.

I nodded, then sighed. "Both were so horrible."

"Mark is probably going out of his mind with worry for his poor dog," she said with a wrinkled frown.

"Actually, I'm not so sure." I shot a glance toward Octo-Cat, who'd seated himself on the opposite side of the table and taken up a vigorous grooming session focused primarily on his forehead and ears.

He paused and nodded his approval.

"Per Octo-Cat, the mayor was lying to us. Or at least hiding something important," I revealed as I played the conversation back through my head.

"About which part?" Nan wondered aloud.

I shook my head, yet again wishing I knew the answer.

She snorted. "Well, that's helpful."

"Still, at least we know to take what little he told us with a giant grain of salt."

Nan considered this, then stood suddenly, flinging her chair backward with such force it startled me and both animals.

"Where are you going?" I asked as she scurried toward the coat closet off the foyer.

She didn't look back as she explained, "If the

mayor isn't going to tell us the truth, then we'll have to go find it for ourselves."

"Online?" I asked meekly even as she'd already begun to pull on her hot-pink snow boots.

"No," she said, shaking her head. "Outside."

Ugh. That was the exact place I wanted to avoid, given our current polar vortex situation.

"I'm not going," Octo-Cat said from his place a few stairs up from the ground floor.

I paused between shoving my mitten on one hand and readying it for the other. "Why not? You always come. You're my partner, after all."

He turned his nose up at me. "Yeah, well, this partner doesn't do subzero temperatures."

"It's still at least five degrees out there. And this isn't some stupid jog, it's part of our investigation. C'mon."

"Let me rephrase that." He paused and took several deep breaths before continuing. "I don't do cold and wet. It's like the whole world decided to take a bath and then let the water grow frigid. I don't do baths. And if my fur coat isn't enough to keep warm, then I'm not going."

"Fine. Then you're not going. But you also better not complain about being left out." I turned away from him and began to dress for the impromptu outing.

"Please. I have better things to do with myself than follow you around on your wild goose chase." He yawned to emphasize his point.

Paisley ran up beside Octo-Cat, wagging her tail so vigorously she stumbled and fell down one of the steps. "Mommy, I'm coming, right?"

"Of course you are!" I assured her.

"Just one last thing and we can go," Nan said, reaching for a plastic shopping bag on the top shelf of the closet and pulling out a baby pink sack. "It's the wrong shade of pink, but it will have to do."

I eyed the cloth accessory warily. "What is it?"

"I'll show you! C'mere, my sweet girl." Nan smacked her lips and bent down to pick up the Chihuahua who came running straight into her arms. She then worked the straps of the sack over her arms so that it rested against her chest.

Paisley realized what was going on about the same time I did and began to wiggle in desperate fright. "No, no, no! I don't want to go in the bag!" she yelped.

"Just hold still for a second, my dear," Nan instructed, wrestling with the Chihuahua to wedge her into the baby carrier.

Paisley continued to whine and squirm.

"Angie, can you please tell her this will be a lot easier if she cooperates?" Nan grunted.

"Sweetie, you need to—" I began, but Nan interrupted with a triumphant "Ah-ha!"

The poor little Chihuahua had been tucked into the carrier and strapped in securely. Only her tiny face and giant ears peeked out from the top.

Nan spun and posed. "What do you think?"

Octo-Cat laughed heartily. "Ha, ha, you look ridiculous!" he crowed.

Paisley whimpered and sighed.

"I'm not so sure she likes it," I offered.

"Well, she just has to get used to it is all. It will help keep her warm while we're out and about. It's made especially for little dogs like her, you know. By the way, you'll have to drive. We can take my car, though."

"Okay," I said and followed my grandmother outside to her car. It was easier to just go along with what she said. At least this wouldn't require any grueling exercise.

Or so I sincerely hoped...

7

M ayor Dennison live in a surprisingly modest house on the far edge of town. Part of me had hoped we'd have housekeepers, cooks, butlers, and a full garrulous staff to question, but just like crime—small-town politics didn't pay.

It was clear Mayor Mark lived alone. It was also clear that nobody was at home. What wasn't clear was how Nan knew where to find him.

"Think we can break in?" she asked now, rifling through her pockets for who knew what.

Paisley heaved a giant sigh from her place affixed to the front of Nan's chest. I had to admit, she looked absolutely adorable in that Puppy Bjorn.

"I'd rather not start our investigation by

committing a B&E," I said. My breath rose above us in icy puffs.

"Look at you with the lingo," Nan crooned, clutching a hand to her chest, or rather to Paisley on her chest. "You don't have to help, but—yeah—I'm breaking in."

I groaned. Of course she was.

Paisley whined and shivered so violently I was surprised that Nan didn't seem to notice.

"Are you okay?" I asked the dogcicle.

"S-S-S-S-So c-c-c-cold," she answered weakly.

"Nan," I called as she moved toward the porch with a sure stride. "Nan, we need to put Paisley back in the car with the heat running."

"N-N-N-N-No," Paisley cried, her eyes practically sealed shut with quick freezing tears. "I w-w-want to h-h-help."

"I'm not letting you catch your death," I promised whether or not she wanted to hear it. "C'mon, I'll take you back to the car."

"Hang on a minute there," Nan muttered. "We'll be inside the house in just a..." She bit her tongue as she maneuvered something in the lock.

"Second," she finished triumphantly and pushed the door open, motioning for me to lead us inside.

Oh, I didn't like this at all. As bad as it was to take part in this unlawful entry, it would have been even worse to send Nan inside unsupervised.

"Five minutes," I hissed between clenched teeth. "Then we go, no matter what."

"Well, you're no fun."

I ignored that last barb and searched the tidy open floor plan for something that might prove useful in our investigation.

"Look for a home office," Nan suggested, already sneaking deeper into the house.

"Hello?" A deep voice called from the top of the staircase, turning my blood cold despite the warm air inside.

My eyes zoomed toward the mayor, who stood in a matching flannel pajama set staring at us with huge, unblinking eyes. "Oh, Mark, hi," I sputtered, unable to rip my eyes away. How were we going to explain this one?

Even though I had no answers, Nan was quick to save the day.

"Didn't you hear us knock?" she asked, bringing both hands to her hips.

The mayor looked back behind him for a second. "No, I was—"

"Well, then you should at least lock your door. Really, anyone could wander in off the streets."

He ran a hand through his hair and then shook his head with a sigh. "You're right. Of course you're right."

We all stood staring at each other for a few silent moments.

Finally Mark spoke up, putting the uncomfortable moment to rest. "Can I, uh, help you with something?"

"We wanted to talk with you a bit more about the... the-the... the case," I explained quickly, stumbling over a few choice words. "We don't have much to go on and thought—"

"I told you everything I know," the mayor interrupted with a scowl. "It's all I have. That's why I hired you to find and put together the rest of the pieces. Are you suggesting you're not up for the task?"

Nan laughed at this. "Oh, we'll handle it. Don't you worry. Your case is as good as solved with Pet Whisperer, P.I."

I still hated that name, but Nan and Mom had both made sure I'd be stuck with it going forward.

Mark straightened to his full height and finally

descended the stairs. "Well, good. That's just what I needed to hear."

"Since we're here," I jumped in smoothly before the mayor could push us out the door. "Would you mind giving us a quick tour as it relates to Marco and his daily schedule? It always helps to get into the victim's head when we can."

"Yes, a tour would be most helpful," Nan agreed, nodding vigorously.

Paisley barked her agreement. The way the carrier shook suggested that she had tried rather unsuccessfully to wag her tail.

"Sure. Okay." Mark shook his head, ran another hand through his hair, then waved for us to follow. What followed was a lengthy description of the missing golden retriever's daily comings and goings, including when and what he ate, where he liked to sleep, his favorite spots to pee in the yard, and more.

"So as I'm sure you can see," the mayor said when the tour concluded, "despite my own busy schedule, Marco was well taken care of and very much loved. Please bring him home safely. And soon."

"We will. We will," Nan assured him.

Personally, I would rather under promise and

overdeliver. "We'll do everything we can," I said as we shook hands goodbye.

Paisley, however, had other, more important things on her mind.

"Marco has good instincts," she whispered in admiration on our way out. "If I lived here, I would choose to pee there, too."

I glanced toward the area on the side of the house the mayor had pointed out mid-way through our tour. The snow was too fresh and too deep to give anything away.

But, well, at least our abducted dog had good taste in pee spots. As for our case, we still had absolutely nothing to go on.

Yet.

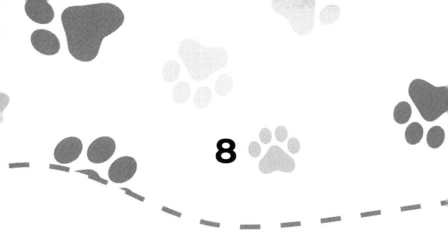

8

"**W**ow, that human really loves his dog," Paisley observed on the drive home. I'd taken her out of the pet carrier as soon as Nan had handed her over to me and settled herself behind the wheel. She'd since repaid me with no less than a few dozen enthusiastic doggie kisses.

Her debt paid, Paisley had now turned her mind back to the investigation. "I feel so sad that they have been separated. We're going to get his dog back soon. Right, Mommy?"

I kissed the small white spot on the Chihuahua's forehead. "Yes, we will."

The little dog wagged her tail and opened her mouth in a panting grin.

Later, Nan sighed as she made the turn into our driveaway. "Well, that accomplished exactly nothing."

"I don't know what you expected. He's our client, not the suspect. Even though I agree with Octo-Cat that he's hiding something. I also agree with Paisley that he really loves that dog."

"So much that he won't give us all the information that we need to get him back?" Nan chuckled and shook her head. "I don't think so."

"Whatever he's hiding, we don't know whether it's related to the ransom," I pointed out as the car bumped along the icy drive.

Finally, Nan parked and the three of us raced inside as fast as our feet would carry us. Octo-Cat sat waiting for us in the center of the coffee table.

"Well?" he asked with one raised eyebrow. "How did the break-in go?"

I stared at him in disbelief. "Who says we broke in?"

"Please. Nan went, so you were bound to break in. It's what she does." He chuckled merrily to himself.

Touché.

"So?" He raised the other eyebrow. "How'd it go?"

"Oh, right. Unfortunately, there's not much to tell. We got caught and then got a very detailed tour and description of Marco's day-to-day routine."

"Yuck. I'm glad I missed that." My cat shuddered, shaking off several loose hairs in the process.

I watched them dance through a nearby sunbeam, entranced.

"We're still at square one," Nan muttered, "but I refuse to stay there."

I watched her shrug out of her winter gear and then reach back into the closet. Sometimes I suspected our foyer closet wasn't unlike Mary Poppins's magical bag. It seemed she never ran out of space and always had exactly what she needed waiting. This time, Nan pulled out poster board, Sharpies, sticky notes, and a pack of little magnifying glass stickers, then dumped them all onto the living room coffee table.

Octo-Cat had to leap out of the way to avoid being buried under the falling heap of craft supplies. "Watch it, old lady!"

I shot him a withering look, then returned my focus to Nan. Unlike my snarky tabby, she at least had a plan—one with flair at that.

She arranged all her supplies just so and then set to work, using a dark green marker to divide the neon green poster board into three evenly spaced sections. Next, she selected the black marker and scrawled People at the top of one column, then Places and Events on the others.

Out came the stickers, which she used to create bullet points, three down each column.

"We'll start with three each, but don't worry, I have enough stickers to match however many ideas we come up with. So what's the first one? How about a person?" Nan stared at me expectantly, a blue marker uncapped and at the ready.

She'd created a similar setup when Octo-Cat had gone missing, so I knew exactly what she expected during today's shared brainstorm.

"Start with his opponent," I directed. "The one he very narrowly beat in the election. He definitely has a grudge."

Nan nodded and wrote the name down. "I'll add Brenda Eaves. She was one of the folks protesting at the inauguration, and if we play our cards right, I bet we can get her to tell us the names of the others, too."

Octo-Cat watched in silence while Paisley snoozed on my lap. Tiny whimpering sighs escaped her muzzle as she dreamed.

"How about—?" I was just about to suggest a

third suspect when a sudden, persistent tapping drew my attention to the window.

Octo-Cat spotted the source before I could and startled me by rearing up to hiss. He hissed often, but very rarely went full into Halloween kitty mode.

I followed his line of sight and found our favorite backyard roommate staring straight back at me with a cheesy smile. "Pringle! What are you doing here?"

He motioned toward his ear and shook his head. The raccoon's mannerisms seemed so human at times and were only becoming more so, given his insane addiction to reality TV.

"I know you can hear me!" I shouted louder.

He shook his head harder.

"Fine!" I threw my hands up and stomped toward the door. The very moment I flung it open, the plump gray ball of fur scuttled inside.

Our primary rule with Pringle was that he was not allowed in the house. He'd committed too much blatant destruction and secret thieving to keep that particular privilege.

"You invited me!" he shouted back over his shoulder without so much as a glance my way. "No takesy-backsies!"

"Noooooo!" Octo-Cat screamed in utter agony. "He's eating my Delectable Delights!"

I sprinted into the kitchen, but the raccoon had already gulped down the whole bowl of crunchies. Normally, Octo-Cat didn't do dry food, but ever since his beloved long-distance girlfriend Grizabella had become the spokesmodel for the new brand, he'd made the difficult choice to switch his loyalty away from Fancy Feast and toward Delectable Delights.

He stumbled into the kitchen and mock-fainted, falling to his side dramatically. The fact that his tail still flicked in irritation was proof enough he hadn't lost consciousness.

Still, I had to agree with him here. Pringle was way out of line.

"I didn't invite you inside," I hissed in the thieving critter's direction.

"You opened the door. Same difference, yeah?" He jumped onto the counter and helped himself to a freshly baked muffin, then stood on his hindlegs and simpered at me with narcissistic joy.

"So what did I miss?" he asked, taking a huge bite and chewing with his mouth open. "Did we have a new case come in?"

"It's not your case!" Paisley barked as she scampered across the tile floor to join us. Then, bless her, she began to jump in a desperate attempt to join the raccoon on the counter. There was no way the diminutive pup would ever reach, but I appreciated her moxie all the same.

So now there we stood in our private domestic calamity.

Paisley barked.

Octo-Cat swooned again, lifting himself slightly from the floor and falling down in a dramatic heap.

Pringle watched both and laughed as he feasted on baked goods.

"Stop dawdling and get back in here!" Nan shouted.

I downed a pair of painkillers for my quickly growing headache and marched back into brainstorm headquarters, AKA my former living room.

All the animals followed, and Nan jumped straight back into business.

"Now we obviously need to return to the mayor's house when we can." She paused and wrote that down. "What other places should we make sure to check as part of our investigation?"

"Ooh! Ooh!" Pringle's hand shot high into the air. "I know! I know! Pick me! Pick me!"

I could scarcely hold back my irritated groan.

Something told me this was going to be a very long and painful afternoon.

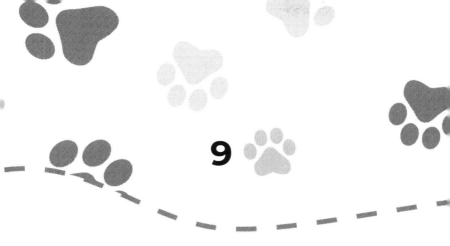

9

had to work hard to hold back my laughter when Pringle marched across the room and ripped the marker right out of Nan's hand.

"I'll take that," he said as he began to scribble at the bottom of the last column, completely ruining Nan's perfectly organized mind map.

He scrawled furiously for close to a minute, then drew away from the board and recapped the marker with a self-satisfied smirk. "There. You're welcome."

I studied the writing closely but couldn't figure out what it was meant to say. We'd famously discovered that Pringle could read when he stole an important letter that revealed long-kept family secrets and turned our world upside-down.

Apparently, though, he didn't possess even minor writing skills. It wasn't just poor penmanship, either. The markings looked more like hieroglyphics than actual letters of the alphabet.

"Um, what's it supposed to say?" I asked at last.

He snorted, then crossed the whole thing out. "If you're going to act like that, you don't deserve my help."

Octo-Cat growled and pounced at the rude raccoon. "Nobody talks to my human like that—nobody except for me!"

"I'm the new and improved you, baby. Deal with it," Pringle spat back, placing a hand on each hip and laughing at the irate feline.

Paisley barked and ran large, looping circles around the other two animals as they prepared to fight.

"Stop! Stop!" I cried, but my pleas fell on deaf ears.

My cat pulled his front paws up and set his ears back flat against his head.

The raccoon drew nearer, stalking on all fours until he was mere inches away, then he rose upright as well.

I held my breath and the moment seemed to freeze in time.

Both combatants stared at each other, unblinking. Each waiting for the other to strike first.

Octo-Cat raised a paw slowly, slowly... and then like lightning he batted Pringle right in the face.

"Oh, no you didn't!" the raccoon shouted and began slapping Octo-Cat in the chest with both hands at rapid speed.

My cat swiped back, landing one strong blow for every ten mini slaps that came from Pringle.

I didn't know what to do.

Part of me wanted to grab a video camera and put this on YouTube to see if we could reach viral fame, but a much larger part was afraid that Octo-Cat would take a solid beating. I couldn't let that happen, especially since this had all started over him coming to my defense.

And then Paisley redirected the path of her latest circle and took a running leap, which landed her right on top of the battling mammals.

"Mommy said stop it!" she barked.

"Really? You sent in the pipsqueak dog?" Pringle shot me a venomous look. "I've never been so insulted in my entire life. I'm outta here."

He marched into the foyer with his nose held so high in the air that he nearly collided with the wall for lack of visibility. The shock of it stopped him dead in his tracks.

I watched dumbfounded as Pringle heaved a few giant breaths, then turned back toward us and came running on all fours. "I'm taking these," he announced before unceremoniously gathering up a handful of markers and the poster board we'd been using to chronicle the case facts and making his final exit—one made far less dramatic by the fact he had to push, pull, yank, and maneuver the poster board in several different directions before finally getting it out through the pet door with him.

"Great. That's just great," Nan groused. "Now we'll have to start all over."

"Let's take a snack break first," I suggested, still unable to believe how far off the rails this activity had already gone.

"I'm okay by the way," Octo-Cat informed me with a sniff. "You could at least show a little concern for your night of shining stars."

I shook my head; unsure I'd heard correctly. "My what?"

The tabby sighed and cast me a disapproving look. "Night of shining stars. You know, your rescuer?"

"My knight in shining armor," I suggested.

"Yeah, whatever. You humans have the weirdest expressions. I see a night of shining stars every day, but I've never seen a knight in shining armor. Have you?"

Well, he had me there.

A change of topic was needed, and fast. "I'm making sandwiches," I announced, heading for the kitchen.

"Turkey for me, please," Nan called after me.

"Me, too!" Octo-Cat added as he trotted after me.

"Me, three!" Paisley cried but remained with Nan.

When I returned with our tray of sandwiches, I found Nan engrossed in some story playing on the local news station.

A vision of my mother, the long-time anchor, filled the screen. She looked lovely today in a lavender blouse and dark pencil skirt. Mayor Mark Dennison sat opposite her in their in-studio interview room.

The ticker at the bottom of the screen revealed: Dognapped! The new mayor's golden retriever is threatened!

"I just can't believe anyone would take out their political frustrations on Marco. He's a great dog and doesn't deserve any of this." He turned toward the camera, eyes full of unshed tears. "Please, if you took my Marco, please bring him back. I'll do anything."

Nan scoffed. "Yeah, anything but resign apparently."

She said it. Pretty much the only thing I knew about our case so far is that I didn't much care for our client.

Why was he doing a publicity interview when he should be out searching for his missing dog?

It just didn't make any sense.

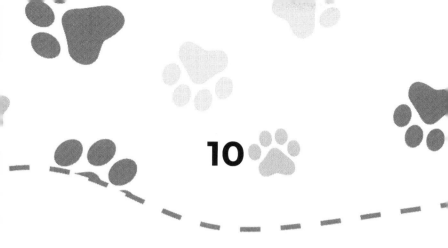

10

fter the discomfiting news interview concluded, Nan switched off the TV and sashayed into the foyer. Apparently we were going out—again. Yes, for the third time that day. This wouldn't bother me so much if the temperature hadn't now dipped south of zero. Brrr.

Paisley pranced after me as I joined Nan at the coat closet. "Where to now?" I groaned.

"To the library!" Nan declared, raising a finger in the air and pointing dramatically toward the ceiling.

I glanced up with a curious expression.

"No, not that library. The public one." Nan looped a brightly colored, hand-knit scarf around her neck, then buttoned up her coat.

"Sorry, girl," I told the eager Chihuahua at my feet. "You're going to have to sit this one out."

"What? Why?" she whined, tucking her tail to cover her privates. "I want to come, too, Mommy."

"No pets at the library," I said with an apologetic shrug. "Besides, it'll be boring."

"Says you," Nan muttered, but luckily Paisley was far too focused on me to notice anything else.

"I'm staying here," Octo-Cat announced a moment later.

"Good, because you're not invited."

"What? No. I want to come," he protested.

Hmm. I'd have to try that reverse psychology trick on him later. For now, though, he honestly couldn't accompany us.

"Sorry," I said even though I didn't really feel it. "Library rules."

Turning to Nan, I mouthed, "go now." We rushed out the door and into the car before either pet could join us.

"What are you hoping to find at GPL?" That's Glendale Public Library, by the way. I'd always been a huge fan, which was why the library and I were on an acronym basis.

Nan shook her head. "Not me, you."

"Okay." I swallowed down my argument. "What am I hoping to find at GPL?"

"You're going to search back issues of all the area papers to see what you can learn about the mayor's past." She checked her hair in the rear-view mirror, then applied a coat of light pink lipstick.

I resisted the urge to check my appearance, mostly because it didn't much matter. "And what are you going to do?"

"I'm going to dig around on those social media sites to see what I can learn about his private life in recent years," my grandmother explained with a grin. Of course, she'd keep the more interesting task for herself.

"Remember," she said after parking outside the squat brick building. We were one of only a handful of cars that had braved the elements to visit the library today. One of them—an old van—looked familiar but I couldn't quite place it.

"Hmm?" I asked, drawing my eyes back toward Nan.

"Remember," she repeated with a sigh. "Same three columns. People, places, events. Jot down anything that sticks out, and we'll reassemble our brainstorm board once we're back home."

"Got it," I said with a quick nod of affirmation.

None of our cases had ever brought us here before, but then again none of our other victims had such a public record as Mayor Mark Dennison.

Even though we'd once investigated the murder of a senator, the circumstances had been totally different. Clues had thrown themselves at us left and right then; we'd never really had the chance to step back and research the history.

Today, Nan made a beeline for the computer bank as soon as we passed through the double glass doors. Since I didn't know quite where to begin with my task, I approached the librarian scanning in books at the main desk. She was young, probably new, given the fact I'd never come across her before —at the library or otherwise.

"Hi there. How can I help you?" she asked with a tight nod.

"I'm looking for back issues of the Blueberry Bay newspapers. Do you have, um, microfiche, I guess?"

Her eyes widened as she took me in a bit more fully. "How far back are you looking to go?"

That was a good question. How far back did I need to go to uncover the mayor's political skeletons? Probably not too far, given his relatively young age.

"How about five years?" I decided at last.

The librarian chuckled as she stepped around the desk and motioned for me to follow her. "You don't need microfiche for that. Everything's digitized these days. C'mon, I'll introduce you to the archives."

She delivered me to the same bank of computers where Nan already sat deep in her research and clicked on an unfamiliar looking icon at the bottom of the screen.

"There," she declared. "This is the homepage for our digital collections. We don't have a lot compared to the fancy big city libraries like Portland or Bangor, but for such a small town, we have a rather impressive collection."

"Thank you," I said, scanning the list of periodicals on the site while the librarian hovered over my shoulder. I'd done some archival research during my college days, but on far broader topics. I'd never looked for something so specific or for something I wasn't even sure I'd be able to find.

The young librarian patted my shoulder and smiled again. "I'll just be at the desk. Give me a whisper if you need anything." With that, she walked away, chuckling to herself.

I scanned headlines starting with this week's

and slowly working back through time. Like the mayor had said, most people who opposed him did so because of his relative lack of experience coupled with his status as a proud bachelor and his narrow win in the election.

I found several letters to the editor that complained about precisely these facts. By noting the names of the letter writers when available and the dates on which the letters were published, I was able to compile quite the list to share during our next group brainstorm.

"Find anything juicy?" Nan asked from across the way using a hushed tone.

I glanced up to find her peering between two of the computers to watch me. "Not much," I admitted.

"Well, then hurry. Come over here. You'll never believe what I just found."

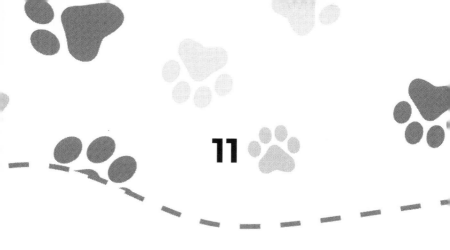

11

turned off the monitor on my computer and walked the long way around the computer bank, bringing myself to hover over Nan's seated form.

She had several different browser windows open; the topmost was Mark Dennison's personal Facebook profile.

"How long have you two been friends?" I asked in surprise.

"Since about twenty minutes ago," she replied with a distracted smile as she pointed to a status toward the bottom of the feed.

I had to hand it to her, she worked fast and effectively.

"Look right here," Nan continued. "This post is

from several years back and about six months before the mayor adopted Marco."

I read over her shoulder:

Should we really elect this candidate just because his wife came down with cancer? Sure, it's sad, but it doesn't change his politics. Vote with logic. Not sympathy.

"What a charmer," I remarked.

"You said it." Nan scrolled back up toward the top of the page. "There are a few other posts commenting on current events in a similar manner, and then—boom!—puppy Marco shows up and takes over his feed."

I blinked hard. "So what do you think that means for our current case?" I asked, not wanting to connect the dots even as they were laid right out before me.

"Well, if you were really unpopular, what would you do to try to boost your own support?" Nan asked with a soft chuckle. "I, of course, can't answer that question, having always been well liked in my day."

I rolled my eyes. Sometimes Nan sounded too much like Octo-Cat for my liking. "Anything else?"

"You can see right here in plain writing that he believes these tactics work whether or not he likes them. And, look, he keeps referring to the new puppy as his family. The lack of a family has been the public's number-one criticism of him ever since he first decided to run for public office. He started with the local school board, I believe. It's the easiest in since there are so many spots."

I hated this. If Nan was right... That poor dog had never been anything more than an extra ballot.

"So you don't think he loves Marco? You think it is some kind of maneuver?"

"If you consider the timing of it all, things certainly look suspicious."

"Suspicious. Right," I said with a sigh. "Everything about this is suspicious. Maybe Octo-Cat is right. Murders are easier than kidnappings."

"For someone who didn't want him to come with us, you're sure talking about that cat a lot." Nan smiled to herself. "Now tell me what you were able to find in the papers."

I swallowed down a lump in my throat. "Nothing. We've only been here a few minutes."

"And yet that was enough time for me to find this golden nugget. Get it? Golden? As in retriever?"

I shook my head, refusing to laugh at such an obvious pun. "Does that mean we're done here?" I asked instead.

"Not quite." Nan closed all the Internet windows and brought up the library's internal search engine. "While we're here I think I'm going to check out a couple of books that have knitting patterns."

Nan never failed to surprise me, and this latest revelation was no exception. "Knitting? I thought you gave that up. You said it was for old ladies, remember?"

"I did, but it's been cold. And I thought EB could use a sweater to help keep her warm."

Ah, EB. Nan's new kind of, sort of boyfriend's pet rabbit. EB was short for Easter Bunny, and that nervous little rabbit had helped us solve our last case—two homicides and a kidnapping, all solved in record time.

Somehow, I didn't think EB would like being restricted by a knit straightjacket, but at least it would keep Nan happy and busy.

"Okay. While you do that, I'll keep searching the newspapers. Surely, there must be something helpful there."

Nan powered down her computer and shuffled into the back of the library.

I closed my eyes, willing something to appear on my screen, something that could help. While I appreciated Nan's theory, I couldn't believe someone would commit to a pet for such a superficial reason as a few extra votes.

I thought back to our conversations with the mayor earlier that day.

Whatever his motivations before, Mark Dennison clearly loved Marco now and wanted nothing more than his safe return... Right?

I flipped through the digital archives for another hour or so. The most interesting thing I found was an old editorial discussing bachelors in politics and how they really weren't suited to the job at hand.

Poor Mark. It seemed the whole world was against him. Part of me felt bad for questioning him about anything. Keeping the truth at least partially concealed came with the job; it was the politician's way. Obviously, the public would use whatever it could take to rake him through the coals, burning or not.

When I'd finished my uneventful research, I found Nan sitting in the Young Adult section chatting with a red-headed girl in braided pigtails. All she needed was a sock monkey and she'd be the perfect likeness of Pippi Longstocking.

While Nan was arguably too old for the literature at hand, Pippi here wasn't quite mature enough. She appeared to be nine years old at the absolute most. Her freckles covered her skin so completely it almost changed the color of her complexion.

"Are you ready to go home?" I asked, feeling like I was my grandmother's mother in this situation.

"Not just yet," Nan said with a higher pitched voice than usual. "Betsy and I here were just discussing the circumstances surrounding Lord Voldemort's second rise to power. Now Betsy, you were saying that Nagini was more than just a snake. Care to extrapolate on that?"

I groaned and turned away. As much as I loved Harry Potter myself, I suspected having a deep discussion with Nan about the lore would take some of the fun out of it for me.

Then again, I did love to read, and I was at a library. Maybe I could have a quick nose around, pick something fun to read for once this case was put to bed.

Although I normally favored novels, I found myself wandering toward the section on unusual pets. I'd been lucky so far with the animals who had inadvertently joined our P.I. Practice, but what would I do if I found an armadillo or a chinchilla or even a ball python wanting to join in and help solve mysteries?

Yes, it was definitely best to be prepared for anything.

Nan came and found me a short while later. "There you are. I've been searching for at least a half an hour."

Funny, because I had left her no more than ten minutes ago. I put the book I'd been thumbing through back on the shelf with its companions and zipped up my coat. "Let's get home then."

There wasn't much to say on the drive back. Nan kept trying to bring things around to her scholarly discussion of Lord Voldemort from the Harry Potter series and even attempted to parallel his rule with that of Mayor Mark Dennison.

Strange, considering how she'd been quick to defend him from the protestors at his inauguration.

Back at home, we found Octo-Cat lying in his usual sunbeam with Paisley nestled up at his side licking the fur on his neck.

Octo-Cat purred loudly and slowly blinked his eyes in contentment. When he noticed us standing there watching them, he jumped up in horror with the same level of absolute shock and disgust he displayed whenever he accidentally found a cucumber laying near him.

What? Sometimes I just couldn't resist.

"So, you and Paisley, huh?" I asked, making a kissy face and widening my eyes dramatically.

"It's not what it looks like, Angela, and you know it. The little dog just needed... Oh why do I bother to explain things to you feeble humans? Get out of here, dog!"

Paisley whimpered and scampered away.

"Do you want to hear about our trip to the library?" I asked, tilting my head to the side.

He stretched his front paws and then stretched his back legs one at a time. Finally Octo-Cat turned to me. "If you must."

I quickly caught him up on what little we'd discovered. I hadn't expected his response to be laughter.

"Oh, you humans, so needy. We cats don't need anybody telling us what to do. We can figure that out for ourselves, thank you very much. In fact, my fourth cousin twenty-three times removed, Stubbs, actually ruled over humans. They elected him to be mayor of their town for twenty years! He served his first term as a kitten, even. And he did a wonderful job. More cats should be mayors, if you ask me. I mean, you see how much better your life is since I've come around to teach you how to live it properly."

"I'm going upstairs," I announced, marching away before Octo-Cat could bore me with any more of his strange family connections or Nan with her far-reaching conspiracy theories.

"Dinner will be ready in an hour," Nan called up after me. "I don't know why, but for some reason I really find myself craving a nice Scotch egg. To the kitchen!"

We both disappeared in opposite directions. It wasn't until I reached my tower bedroom that I realized Paisley had trailed me there.

"Mommy," she said sweetly, wagging her tail and blinking up at me with eyes that always seemed to have tears in them even when she was happy. "I missed you today, Mommy."

"I missed you, too, sweetie. But it was very nice coming home to see you and Octo-Cat getting along so nicely."

"Yeah, but then he hurt my feelings," she whined. "Why does he do that?"

"Oh, sweetie." If only I knew the answer to that question, I could set up a second business as a cat behaviorist and make millions.

12

I spent much of that night tossing and turning as I replayed my conversations with the mayor and Nan's suspicions regarding his motives as a pet owner. Clearly I was missing something big... But what?

That question kept me from entering the deep sleep I so desperately needed.

Octo-Cat quickly grew frustrated with me and went to sleep somewhere else in the house. I missed his warm presence in bed, but it beat listening to him complain about my anxious insomnia.

I'd hoped to sleep in a little the next morning, but Nan would hear of no such thing. As soon as light began peeking from beneath the curtain, she burst in with Paisley yapping at her heels. "Good morning! It's a great day for a run! Our second run! You're going to feel terrible," she said with a sinister smile, "but we have to keep going and then you'll feel great. No time to waste. Chop, chop!"

I pulled the pillow over my head, not caring if it smothered me. Nothing could be worse than running with Nan on almost no shut-eye.

Then Octo-Cat, proving things could always get worse, appeared with a dead rat in his mouth and dropped it directly on me.

I shrieked and pushed the covers, and the rat, to the ground. Paisley quickly zoomed in and took possession of the deceased rodent.

"This is yummy! What a big fat rat." Her voice came out muffled, but undeniably glad.

"Why would you do that to me first thing in the morning? Why would you do that at all?" I asked Octo-Cat, still shivering with disgust.

"Consider it payment. Not a gift. I need something."

"I don't want it as a gift or a payment! I don't want it at all!" I shuddered again. These little gifts —or payments—of his were made that much worse by the fact I could talk to rats, too.

Octo-Cat never minded making me uncomfortable, though. All that mattered was his own needs.

"You really made me uncomfortable last night, Angela," he began with a sigh. See?

"With all that tossing and turning and mumbling in your sleep, I could scarcely catch any winks myself. That just won't do. I need my own bedroom. My own bed."

"You've got to be kidding me. I can't handle this right now. Nan, I don't feel well. I can't go for the run. I need to save all my energy for the case."

She waved away my concern. "Nothing like getting your blood pumping first thing in the morning to wake up that tired brain."

I groaned. Why couldn't they leave me alone for just five minutes? Was that so much to ask? Five minutes would help so much.

"I'm guessing there's no way out of this?"

"Nope," Nan answered pertly and then tossed a water bottle my way. I didn't catch it. Instead, it bounced back to the floor.

Paisley had already left the room, rat in mouth, which I desperately hoped I wouldn't be seeing again. I also would not be letting Paisley lick me until she had a good solid teeth-brushing.

"Let's go. Hurry up," Nan said, taking her role as my personal trainer far too seriously.

Octo-Cat jumped on the bed and stared daggers

at me through his amber eyes. "Seeing as you accepted my payment, I'll expect services to be rendered by nightfall. Don't forget. When you get home, I get my own bedroom and it better be a nice one. This is my house, after all."

I ignored him as I got ready for what I already knew would be a terribly exhausting day.

Paisley was still off somewhere with my rat payment, making it easy to sneak away without her. Unfortunately, we still had far too much snow for her to be safe and warm outside.

For both of our sakes, I hoped the weather improved soon, but I knew better than to expect that of Blueberry Bay in early February.

Nan drove us to Cujo's house, then grabbed him from the side yard and clipped on his leash.

"I expect you to do better today." The disapproving muttsky narrowed his eerie eyes at me. "Yesterday's performance was unacceptable, but I'm glad you're here to try again. We'll make a runner of you yet."

"I don't know why it's so important to you," I mumbled. "You don't even know me."

"Oh, but I know running," Cujo answered with a chuckle as he kicked his legs back in the snow.

And just like that, we were off.

"So," Nan said as we rounded the first block. "I still think there's something fishy going on about that missing golden retriever."

I knew I wouldn't be able to run in peace. Even small miracles were denied me as of late, it seemed.

"What's this now? A missing retriever?" Cujo asked, still running at breakneck speed.

I, for one, felt as though my shoulder might pop clear out of the socket as I tried to maintain my grip on Cujo's leash and keep pace with both him and Nan.

"Yes," I panted, already overexerted. "It's our case."

"Case?" He asked, his ears twitching and turning with interest.

"I'm a private investigator."

Gasp.

"Me and my..."

Gasp.

"Cat."

He snorted. "You can't give a cat a job. Cat doesn't care about getting it done. You need a dog. Luckily, I volunteer. You give me a job, and I'll get it done. That's what we working breeds do best. So tell me, how can I find this missing golden retriever?"

"What's he saying?" Nan asked and I remembered that while she couldn't make out the words, she could hear the barking and guttural noises uttered by Cujo and other animals as we conversed.

"He wants to help find Marco," I explained, taking several deep gasps for air yet again.

"Perfect!" Nan replied in her normal, unfatigued voice. Here I was about to drop dead and she hadn't even worked up a sweat.

"We'll head straight to the mayor's after we finish our run," she decided aloud.

"No. Please no. I need to rest," I begged. "It's too much all at once. "

"There you go. Disappointing me again," Cujo remarked with a soft growl. "Yes. You definitely need me on this case. I'm part husky, you know. And part Akita and even part Great Pyrenees. All the great strong breeds combined in one. That makes me the greatest."

Wow, this dog had quite the ego. As much as he didn't like cats, he actually reminded me of one.

I hesitated. "I didn't say you were hired."

It seemed to me having to look after Cujo would make the investigation more difficult.

"Of course he's hired!" Nan cried merrily. "Good boy. You tell us how you want your payment, and we'll make sure to get it to you. Do you like rawhides or bully sticks? What can we give you?"

I translated this to Cujo who sighed and said, "A job well done is payment enough, but it's nice to be appreciated."

He glanced over his shoulder and gave me a disapproving look before continuing. "Catch me up on the case so that I'm ready. I'll solve this in record time. You'll see."

I found it quite difficult to relay the facts while continuing our horrible run—but somehow, just barely, I managed. When we finished forty minutes later, rather than yesterday's thirty, I crumpled into the snow, content to die right there so I could finally get some rest.

"What are you doing?" Nan asked with a laugh.

Cujo was far less amused. "Get up! Now is not the time to be lazy. We can't rest until the job is done."

I made a snow angel, ignoring them both until my heart finally slowed to a steadier beat. Moderately refreshed, I got up and dutifully headed to the car

"Now that wasn't so bad. Was it?" Nan asked as she ushered Cujo into the tiny back seat. It barely contained his one hundred pounds of fluffy bulk, but he didn't seem to mind.

I laughed a bitter laugh and closed my eyes, leaning back on the headrest.

The sooner we solved this case, the sooner I could return to trying to get some shut-eye. Hopefully by the time we returned home, Octo-Cat would have forgotten all about his demand for a new bedroom.

Then again, when had he ever forgotten about anything? Or at least anything that concerned him?

13

Nan, Cujo, and I arrived at the mayor's house for the second time in two days. I had an uneasy feeling about snooping around, sorely hoping Nan didn't plan on breaking and entering today as well.

We'd been lucky enough to explain our unexpected presence yesterday, but if Mark caught us today, he would surely figure out that we were investigating him just as much as the disappearance of his dog.

"Is that the mark?" Cujo asked, panting heavily beside me. He'd stuffed his giant slobbery face between the two front seats and over the armrest. Funny that he didn't get winded at all during the run, but this new excitement of the investigation

had his tongue lolling freely from his enormous
maw.

I scanned the horizon just in time to see the
mayor pulling away in his luxury sedan.

"I'll tail him," Nan said, nudging me in the ribs.
"Get out. You can look around here, and I'll follow
him wherever he's going."

As tired as I was, I also knew better than to
argue. At least I'd be able to move at my own
pace now.

But no.

A moment later, I found myself standing in the
fresh snowfall with Cujo at my side. "Why didn't
you stay with Nan?" I asked him, not so secretly
wishing he had.

"And miss all the action? No thank you. I hate
that metal dogsled, anyway. I'm supposed to be
pulling, not sitting." He chuffed and pawed at the
snow impatiently.

"Well, c'mon then." I tromped up the unshov-
eled drive. I'd have thought the mayor would
ensure his home was one of the first on the local
snowplow's route. Then again, it was probably hard
for the city to keep up, given the record-breaking
snowfall Glendale had seen during the past week.

"What are we looking for?" Cujo asked. "I don't

like standing here wasting time. Not when we have a job to do."

I'd only stopped for a few seconds, but apparently that was long enough for the hyperactive work hound. "I'm not sure," I answered, bracing myself for the insults I had no doubt would be coming.

Luckily, whatever he'd been about to say died on Cujo's lips as a frigid blast of wind crashed into us face-on.

"Ah, that feels good," he said with a happy sigh, then his entire body stiffened as he took a long, exaggerated whiff of the air.

"I smell something," he informed me.

"Smell something, like what?"

"Pee."

Oh, great. "Yeah, um, we were here yesterday for a tour, and the mayor pointed out that Marco always peed on that side of the yard."

"No, that's not right." Cujo barked and turned his head in the opposite direction. "It's coming from over there!"

He pointed toward the woods, one paw raised mid-step.

"Are you sure? Nothing's back there," I explained.

"So trusting, you humans. I'd wager a healthy bit of skepticism is just as important to a private investigator as a snow hook is to a musher. At least it should be."

"Oh…kay," I said slowly, neither wanting nor knowing how to argue this point with him.

Cujo whined against his leash. "We need to go to the pee. It will tell us everything we need to know."

Wonderful. Still, at least it was something.

We plodded along much slower than Cujo would have liked until we were deep into the woods. Even though the sun was still high, the tall, aged trees cast shadows over us.

"I'm not so sure about this," I told him, taking out my phone and noting that my reception was down to one bar. "Nobody knows we're back here. What if…?"

Cujo interrupted me with a low growl. "No time for what-ifs. We have a case to solve. Have you forgotten already?"

I had two choices.

I could disappoint the very large, very angry-looking dog beside me, or I could take the small risk of heading deeper into the woods.

This time, I chose to go into the unknown, following the tireless muttsky through the trees.

By the time we emerged on the other side, I realized that Cujo's keen sense of smell had, in fact, led us somewhere new. A small log cabin sat nestled among the trees on the outer edge of the woods. It probably wouldn't have been visible, if not for the stark white snow that surrounded it. Smoke rose up from the chimney, and a faded trail of footprints led straight to the front door.

It looked like the perfect place to escape the cold and rest for a moment. Oh, how nice that sounded.

"The trail stops here," Cujo informed me, bounding up to the cabin, then lifting a leg and relieving himself with great satisfaction. "There. No more strange dog's pee."

"Is it Marco's? Do you think?" I asked, unfamiliar with the intricacies of dog pee.

"I've never met him, so I can't say for sure." Cujo blinked slowly in the sunlight. "But let me see..."

He stuck his snout in the snow. "This dog is male, about five or six years old, slightly overweight and enjoys snap peas as a snack. Not my favorite but..."

"Interesting," I said, thinking back over the mayor's tour of his home and our discussion of Marco's day-to-day routine. "Oh, wait. I remember something. The mayor did say that he used snap peas as snacks for Marco to help get his weight down since the meat ones were making him too fat."

"Well, then it seems we've found our dog," Cujo answered with a gaping smile. "I told you it was easy when you focused on the task to be done."

He was right. I wouldn't have found this place without him, but still we had to face whatever was inside.

I pushed my body flat against the wall and slowly snuck toward the window. A quick peek inside confirmed that the cabin wasn't sitting empty. A portly golden retriever sat gnawing on a rawhide bone in front of a blazing fire.

"That's got to be him!" I cried, then covered my mouth with my hands, realizing I may have spoken too loudly to avoid detection. The dog's ears perked up, but he didn't move his eyes from the bone. When no one came out to investigate, I realized that Marco must be sitting alone.

"What should we do?" I asked Cujo.

"Go in and rescue him, obviously," Cujo said

with a chuff. "It's the final part of our mission. You can't back off now."

I tried the door, but it was locked. "Any other ideas?" I asked.

"Fall back!" The muttsky jumped to the side, urging me to follow.

Sure enough, in the distance I spotted an approaching figure wearing a Russian fur shapka and thick mittens.

I leapt behind the cabin with Cujo and watched in horror as Mayor Mark Dennison himself finished the trek to the cabin and let himself inside. Could it be?

I carefully, painfully duck-walked to the window and peeked over the ledge. The mayor had settled himself beside his dog and was discussing the case—the one he'd hired us to solve.

I could barely make out his words.

"Well," the mayor said with a chuckle, "the first few interviews went great. My public approval rating must be soaring now. Not only does everybody remember that I have a great dog."

He paused to scratch Marco between the ears. "But they also feel genuinely sorry for me. It's one thing to disagree with my politics, but to take such a nice dog... Who would do such a wicked thing?"

Marco cocked his head to the side and Mark laughed again.

"Yes, it would take someone truly awful." He continued to laugh as the answer to our predicament finally became crystal clear.

No one had ever threatened Marco. The mayor had taken the dog himself and hidden him back here just long enough to get the public sympathy working in his favor.

So what was I supposed to do now?

Barge in and tell him he'd been found out?

He was the client after all, and the one responsible for paying us when the job was done.

Did a little ill-gotten publicity really hurt anyone?

The dog was clearly fine and happy.

So...

Was it better to walk away or to force a confrontation? Before I could decide, Mark let himself back out through the door and clomped away.

I held my breath, praying hard that he wouldn't turn around and see me.

14

I waited crouched in the snow outside that cabin for at least ten minutes, needing to make sure the mayor had well and truly gone before I headed back through the woods with Cujo.

"What's next? What's next? I'm ready for the next part," he begged, panting happily as he led me across the frigid February landscape.

I had to admit that he made a far more motivational partner than the crabby tabby I usually worked beside.

"That's a good question," I told him. "I still haven't decided. What do you think?"

Honestly I was torn. Should we confront the mayor with what we know? Or would it be better for me to call my news anchor mom so she could break the story and expose this scandal to the public? She'd definitely be happy to have such a juicy story. The network execs would be, too. They might even extend her coverage region over something like this.

Cujo stopped walking and stared up at me with his light blue eyes. "I don't care what you do. We found the culprit. It's up to you to navigate the intricacies of human propriety. Not me."

"Uhh....sure," I said in defeat. "Thanks for the help."

"Don't mention it," he yipped.

We walked silently through the woods for a while, neither having anything to say to the other. When we'd almost reached the clearing on the other side, my phone let out a series of high-pitched chirps.

"What was that?" Cujo asked in a panic. "That didn't sound good."

"Relax. It's just my phone." I pulled it out from where it had been wedged in my pants pocket and saw a missed text and two missed voicemails from Nan.

I listened to the first message. "I don't know where you are, Angie dear, but take cover. Mark's headed back your way."

The next voicemail was much the same. Although it definitely would have been nice to have advance warning, it was probably a good thing my phone hadn't chimed and given me away while I was spying through the cabin window.

I tried returning Nan's call to let her know I was okay, but the phone just rang and rang without stop. Meanwhile Cujo and I crept closer to the edge of the forest. I was so ready to get back into the warmth of Nan's car and hoped she'd be nearby and waiting for us.

"What's that?" Cujo asked again.

I turned but saw nothing—nothing except a gloved fist flying straight toward my face. It made contact, crunching my nose and forcing me down into the soft snow below.

Cujo growled, sounding more like his namesake than ever.

"Who's there?" I called, rubbing stars from my eyes, only to be kicked in my side for my efforts. The fresh wave of searing hot pain distracted me from all else.

Cujo lashed out with a snarl, and my attacker screamed in pain. I assumed he had landed his bite. I definitely didn't envy whoever had been on the other end of those giant teeth.

A large thud sounded nearby, and Cujo yelped in response.

"Get out of here, you stupid dog!" I heard someone yell, still too delirious from pain to determine whether the voice had come from a man or a woman.

And then I was alone with my attacker.

Cujo's familiar pant receded, leaving me to handle the assailant all on my own.

"Get up, Russo," he commanded, yanking me to my feet by my hair. A man. Definitely a man, and a strong one, too.

Everything hurt so bad I couldn't help but cry out. "What do you want? Leave me alone!"

"We already told you what we want, but you couldn't keep your nose out of our business," the man told me, but I couldn't make any sense of it.

"Again," another voice added. This one seemed to belong to a woman.

"You're coming with us," the man said, yanking me again.

Everything looked as if it were under water or part of a mirage. I strained to make out the features of either thug, but one them pushed a soft knit skullcap onto my head and yanked it down over my eyes.

"You move that, you're dead," the woman said, and I knew better than to test her on that.

"March," the man said, pushing me from behind. The woman walked just before me.

We turned around and headed back through the woods toward that lonesome cabin. Was this how I died?

Marching blindly through the cold at the hands of an unknown pair who hated me enough to kidnap me? Not just once, but twice now?

I had no doubt in my mind that this was the same duo that had abducted Mags just a month earlier at the Holiday Spectacular downtown. She said they called her Russo and warned her to keep her nose out of their business, just like these two were doing with me now.

What did they have to do with the mayor and his missing golden retriever, though? I'd already seen that he'd taken the dog himself. That neither of them had ever been in any real danger.

Yet here I was, blindfolded and being marched to an unknown end. My bones rattled from the icy cold. My heart hammered with fear—too bad it wasn't quite enough to get me warm.

If I ran, I wouldn't get far—not with these two

around and with my vision already so disoriented, whether or not I was blindfolded.

And if I stopped moving, who knew what they would do to punish me?

This left no option but to comply, so back to the cabin we went.

Sometime later they shattered the window, then unlocked the door and shoved me inside. The warmth of the fire immediately put me at ease despite the ongoing danger.

My kidnappers whispered hurriedly between themselves before finally tugging off the cap that had blinded me.

Marco the golden retriever stood nearby, his tail covering his privates as he whined questioningly. "Who are you?" he asked in a friendly yet fearful voice. "Why have you come to my playhouse?"

I wished I could answer him, but I still didn't know who my attackers were or what they wanted. I had to play it safe. So I addressed them instead, hoping Marco would understand.

"Why are you here? Why am I here? What do you want?" I asked the questions in rapid fire, my jaw throbbing from where I'd been hit, blood gushing from my nose into my mouth. It was probably broken for all I knew. Maybe Mags could teach me a makeup trick or two if I even managed to get out of this alive.

But now I saw clearly that the first of my captors was a woman in her mid-fifties with elegantly coiffed hair and an expensive looking jacket. She seemed familiar, though I couldn't exactly place her.

The man stood in front of the fire with his back to us, saying nothing as he let his partner make an attempt to answer my questions.

"You already know who we are. Why you're here has yet to be determined. What we'll do with you... Huh." She laughed but didn't bother finishing her answer.

I swallowed down a nervous lump that had formed in my throat. Were they really crazy enough to kill me? For what? Sure I'd put a few bad guys behind bars in my time as a PI, but—

"What are you thinking, Russo?" the man said, turning toward me suddenly.

Oh. This face I knew very well. His wrinkled skin had been pulled taut from an apparent cosmetic surgery. The white hair and strong jaw, though, looked the same as ever.

"Mr. Thompson?" I asked as all the pieces began clicking into place. Could it really be my former boss, the partner at the law firm now headed by my boyfriend, Charles Longfellow, III?

"The very same," he said with a hideous smile.

"Why would you do this?" I squinted my eyes and willed myself to see anything but the horrible scene unfolding right before me. "And shouldn't you be in jail?"

He chuckled again, this time bitterly. "You don't do a very good job following up on your cases. Do you think they were going to hold me because some lady got hurt by her cats? No. My lawyer got me out of that one with a slap on the wrist and an accidental death decision. Minimal time served. Now I'm back, and I'm not leaving again. "

It still didn't make sense. "But what do you want? Why come back here? Why follow me?"

"You think we followed you?" the woman asked, shaking her head. "Think again. You just happened to show up."

"I don't understand."

"What's new," Thompson sneered. "You were a lousy paralegal, so it makes sense that now you're a lousy P.I."

I wouldn't just sit here and take this abuse, both physical and mental. My time with Thompson had been served. That wasn't my job anymore. Now I was my own boss.

As far as I was concerned, he could spend the rest of his life behind bars. It's what he deserved, and it's what I would make sure happened.

Just as soon as I figured out how to get away.

15

Thompson forced me down into a wheeled desk chair and used a coarse stretch of rope to tie my hands behind me.

Ouch. That hurts," I complained, which only made Thompson pull harder.

Satisfied with his work, he turned to me again. "Finally you get what's coming to you," he hissed.

"I don't understand," I muttered, trying hard not to sound as desperate as I felt. "I get why you don't like me, but what does that have to do with the mayor or his dog?"

Thompson chuckled and shook his head. "Denise," he addressed the woman who I now assumed to be his wife. "Go find that camera we stashed in the pack, just in case. Looks like it will come in handy, after all."

"On it," she replied and shuffled to the other side of the small cabin, passing the golden retriever as she did.

Marco glanced at up at her briefly, then returned immediately to his rawhide. Some help he was going to be.

"We had no idea we'd find you on our way here," my former boss said. "That was definitely a lucky break. As for the mayor, we didn't kidnap his stupid dog. But from watching his interviews on the local news, it was very obvious that he'd staged the whole thing himself."

I sucked in a sharp breath. How had Thompson figured this out before me? And why did it even matter to him?

His eyes bore into me as he studied my expression. "You always did wear your heart right on your sleeve. You know that? I can see those wheels turning from all the way over here. Yes, anyone with half a brain should have been able to figure out what Mark did. He never did do a good job hiding his... shall we say... loose ethics."

I still didn't get what he was playing at. "But

what does that have to do with you? Why intervene at all?"

"Oh, that's easy," Denise answered for him, returning with the plastic camera in her hands. "Mark Dennison is a terrible mayor, and he never should have been voted in at all."

"And let me guess, you should have," I spat at Thompson.

He sighed. "No. Unfortunately even with my minor record, I'd never be able to hold office now. Denise on the other hand..."

He glanced over my shoulder and smiled as his wife closed the distance between them. They shared a sickeningly sweet victory kiss. Something much too maudlin for kidnapping thieves, if you asked me.

"I'm going to tell everyone what happened when I get out of here," I promised them both, wishing I could shake my fist to emphasize the point. My hands, however, were still tied uselessly behind my back.

"That's where you're wrong," Thompson informed me. He held the camera up and clicked a button. The flash glared bright in my eyes, and a second later, a Polaroid image popped out.

The picture slowly beginning to emerge from the milky film, and just as I had suspected, my nose had definitely been broken. Blood covered the lower half of my face and I looked as if I'd already lost, but I hadn't given up hope yet.

Somehow I would get out of this.

I had to.

After all, what kind of world did we live in if the good guys didn't win in the end? And make no bones about it, I was definitely the good guy in this situation.

"Nice photo." I forced a smirk, hoping to come across as confident. "Got a frame?"

"Quiet," Denise shouted as she slapped me across the back of the head. "We're in charge here, not you," she reminded me.

As if I'd forgotten.

When I turned in search of Thompson, I found him standing by the door, shrugging back into his winter wear. I didn't know where he was going, but I certainly liked my odds better having only Denise to contend with.

No one said anything as he finished getting ready and then departed with the photo in hand.

Denise came around and hopped onto the desk, crossing her legs at the knee as she eyed me.

"I bet you're wondering where he went." She smiled at me, taking her time with this revelation. "Well, that's the exciting part. The dog may not have been enough to make Dennison resign, but you certainly will be. So thank you for stumbling into our perfect little crime scene here."

"What are you going to do?" I asked through gritted teeth. "Threaten to kill me if he doesn't resign?"

"Oh no, that would still leave too many loose ends." Denise took a deep breath, then lowered her gaze to meet mine. "We are going to threaten to kill you if he doesn't resign, and then once he resigns, we'll kill you anyway."

She paused to let that sink in, and a shiver tore through my body. I could tell she meant business. "So either way I don't get out of this alive," I summarized for us both.

"Precisely," came her unfeeling response. She lowered herself back to the floor and winced in pain.

My eyes traveled down the length of her pants, where I found that the hem on one leg was torn and bloodied.

She caught me looking and raised the pant leg to show me the nasty wound that had marred her milky skin. "That stupid dog of yours. He didn't have to bite me."

I was glad he had as I watched her hobble through the cabin in search of something. Maybe it would be enough to give me a fighting chance, if only I could escape my bonds before Mr. Thompson returned.

"This will do nicely," Denise said with a satisfied huff. I twisted myself around in the wheeled chair to watch as she pulled a bottle of Glenlivet from a glass cabinet. "Very nicely, indeed."

She brought the bottle and a large shot glass back to the armchair by the fire and took a seat with them clutched in either hand.

"Want some?" she asked with a cruel laugh as she filled her glass and downed the first shot. "Now there's a painkiller I can get behind," she said with a happy sigh.

I could use a painkiller too, but more than anything I could use this as an opportunity. If Denise drank enough of her self-professed medicine to hamper her senses, then I would have her injured and drunk while my mind remained sharp ready to fight for my life.

She poured herself another shot, savoring this one with tiny, discerning sips.

"I never hated you that much," she revealed. "Sure, my husband had always insisted that you were useless even before the senator's unfortunate end, but I saw you more as clueless rather than incompetent. Not that there's much difference in the end, I guess." She shrugged and finished the liquor in her glass.

If I could keep her talking then I could probably keep her drinking. And the surest way to keep any conversation going was to get the other person to talk about herself, of course.

"Must be hard having your husband be tried and convicted of accidental death."

She shrugged again. "It's a small charge. But yes, it wasn't easy to undergo all that public scrutiny while the case was on."

I nodded. "So that's why you have to make sure to tie up all your loose ends. So that no one has any reason to question you ever again, especially once you yourself step in to run for office."

She pointed at me and made a clicking sound. "You're definitely smarter than my husband claims. I'll give you that."

I watched as she poured a third shot, smiling to myself without saying anything in response.

Yes, I was definitely smarter.

But was I smart enough to wiggle my way out of this one alive?

16

Denise downed another shot, and then considered her bottle of Scotch with a frown. "Not much left. I guess I should've paced myself," she remarked with a snort.

"How is your pain?" I asked kindly, hoping she wouldn't question my motives.

My inebriated captor pulled up her pant leg and moved her ankle from side to side. "Can't even feel it now," she chuffed. "A good liquor is better than any pill, I'm telling you."

I decided to take a chance knowing there wasn't much hope of it paying off. But if it did...

"Now that you're feeling a bit better, I don't suppose you'd untie me?" I asked with an innocent smile.

Denise shook her head and slammed the shot glass onto a side table "Untie you? What do you think? I'm stupid? He said to leave you exactly as you are until he comes back."

"Who's in charge here?" I pressed. "I don't see him anywhere. Do you?"

She sucked air in through her teeth. "No can do, and stop trying to trick me. You think that just because I have a couple drinks in me that sudden-ly..." Her words fell away as a scratching sound by the door caught both of our attention.

There Marco stood, whimpering and dragging his claws along the wooden door frame.

"What is it, boy?" I asked, hope sparking in me anew. "Do you need to go outside?"

Turning back to Denise, I said, "If you just untie me, I can—"

"No way!" she shouted. "I'll take the stupid dog myself."

She turned behind her and glanced to either side. "I don't suppose you saw a leash somewhere around here, did you?"

I shook my head and watched as Denise grew increasingly frustrated with what was quickly proving to be a fruitless search. "You know," I offered slyly. "The rope on my hands would make a mighty good leash. If you just untie me, I could—"

"No." She kicked at my chair. "Stop asking to be untied. It's not going to happen."

"What if I have to go to the bathroom?" I questioned in my last-ditch effort to gain freedom.

"If you have to go to the bathroom," Denise told me with a cruel chuckle. "You can go right were you're seated."

"Gross," I muttered. I'd already heard enough about pee to last a lifetime, thanks to Cujo's preferred method of tracking Marco earlier. The last thing I wanted was to sit in a puddle of my own making while waiting to die.

Marco whined again, twirling in a frantic circle as he begged to be let out. "I have to go! I have to go number two!" he barked. "I can't hold it inside, and I'll be in such trouble if I go on the carpet here. Please! You've got to let me out!"

I glanced toward Denise, knowing she had understood enough to make out the dog's desperation.

"Fine, you stupid mutt," she said to the purebred retriever as she grabbed his collar and led him outside sans leash.

I watched through the broken window as Marco

sniffed around the yard with Denise following closely behind. It didn't take long for him to find a place and squat down, forming an inelegant arc with his back.

Denise let go and took a giant step back. This was my chance.

"Marco!" I yelled. "Go get help!"

She didn't have to know that I could talk to animals to get upset by my latest attempt at escape.

The golden retriever kept his eyes glued on me as he finished going potty. Once finished, he finally spoke his answer. "Why do we need help? We have everything we need at the cabin. It's a nice place for a little break."

Denise grabbed him by the collar and pulled him back through the door.

"That was stupid," she hissed at me. "Try something like that again and I'll move up your date with destiny."

"What? Kill me now instead of later?" I shot back with a scoff.

"That's exactly what I mean," she spat. "Anyway, this stupid dog's not going to help you, so give up on that now."

"What makes you so sure?" I challenged her, raising one eyebrow.

Denise paced over to the mantle and grabbed a bag of Pupperoni. I clearly remembered the Mayor saying that Marco only ate snap peas as a snack, so the Thompsons must've brought this along with them.

Marco immediately sat at attention, thumping his tail against the floor. "Ohhh! Meat treat! Meat treats are the best! I haven't had one for years. Maybe even one-hundred years! Can I have that one? Oh, please, please, please.

He licked his chops as Denise pulled a treat from the bag.

"Do a trick or something," she told him, clearly not an experienced dog owner.

Still, Marco whined, turned in a circle, waved, sat, laid down, crawled, and then rolled over.

Denise laughed and tossed the treat to him.

He caught it easily and finished the entire thing in one big gulp "Another one?" he asked, repeating the lineup of tricks a second time.

Denise gave him a second treat, then put the bag back on the mantle.

"See?" she told me with a smug expression. "She who controls the treats controls the dog, especially with a fat one like this."

I was happy for Marco's sake that he couldn't

understand. Things were bad enough without her insulting his weight.

Denise returned to the overstuffed armchair with Marco following closely at her heels. He panted while staring at her lovingly as she poured another shot from the green bottle, emptying it completely now.

"Shame," she remarked, swirling the last of the liquid gently in her glass.

Marco gave up waiting and flopped down at her feet with a sigh. I was running out of ideas on what to do here. Unfortunately, if I waited much longer she would start to regain her sobriety, and that would make my escape efforts significantly more difficult.

It was at that moment, I found myself wondering what Octo-Cat would do.

Yes, just like those WWJD bracelets that had been so popular in my childhood. What would Jesus do?

Finding myself faced with death, I chose instead to question the wisdom of my talking cat partner. He wouldn't take this kind of disrespect lying down.

That was for sure.

What wasn't for sure is how he would escape

the situation if he found himself in my place. My odds of survival would have been much better if he'd accompanied me today instead of Cujo.

And thinking of the Muttsky raised even more questions.

Where had he gone after the attack?

And for that matter, where was Nan? Did she know I was in danger or how to find me?

Cujo was the only one who knew I'd been taken. Would he come back to save the day? Or did he prefer other more running-based jobs instead?

Unfortunately, there wasn't much I could do to save myself here. I'd try my best, but...

After I'd been stuck in my thoughts for quite some time, a grunting snore from Denise startled me from my frantic internal monologue.

Nice. While I was literally contemplating my death, she was sleeping like a happy, drunken baby.

And did she always snore like a steam engine rushing down the tracks or was her drunkenness to blame?

I watched in silence for a couple minutes just to make sure her sleep was deep, then began fiddling with the rope around my hands. It was tight and even twisting my wrist the smallest degree caused enormous pain.

Still, if it was the only way to escape, I'd need to be brave and weather whatever injuries came from wrestling these ropes. I continued to twist and turn, biting my lip to prevent myself from crying out.

I could do this.

I had to.

And I almost had it, too, when the abrupt sound of the phone ringing brought me to a dead stop.

I thought I'd lost service back in the woods... But no. Thank goodness for small miracles!

Who could be calling now, and would that person prove to be my salvation?

17

Unfortunately I'd had it right the first time. My phone was still out of service range. It was Denise's that had just rung. If I got out of this alive, I'd definitely need to switch carriers.

Denise awakened with a start and fumbled to answer. "Hello?"

She listened for a moment, then said, "Hang on, I can barely hear you. I'm putting you on speaker."

I thanked my lucky stars for stupid criminals.

"Can you hear me now?" Mr. Thompson's voice rang out loud and clear.

"Yes, that's better," Denise answered with a relieved sigh. "Now what were you saying?"

I pretended that I wasn't paying attention by

focusing my gazing toward the window. Really though, I sat taking in every single word.

"We really got lucky running into Russo like we did," Thompson said on the other end of the call. "Dennison's already agreed to resign as long as we let the girl go."

"We agreed to that?" Denise questioned; her words slurred from drink.

"I made sure not to state those exact terms," Thompson added with a cruel laugh.

Denise laughed, too, but it didn't seem to reach her eyes. Was it possible she could be undergoing a change of heart?

I could only hope.

Thompson continued. "He'll be going on the five o'clock news to tender his resignation live. One last publicity stunt before he goes out with a bang," he added, placing eerie emphasis on that final word.

Denise squirmed uncomfortably.

"You have the gun, right?" Thompson asked after a brief pause.

"Yes," she said, quietly pushing herself to her feet. "It's been right here beside me the whole time." She began to search the cabin for what I assumed was the weapon in question.

"Good. Keep it on you in case she gets feisty.

You never know with that one." Thompson paused, but his wife didn't say anything in response as she continued her search.

"I'm going to stay nearby to keep watch," he informed his partner in crime. "Just in case that fool Dennison tries to contact someone for help. I've already threatened to expose his false kidnapping, but he might still be stupid enough to try and double-cross us. Speaking of, keep a close eye on that door. He may try sneaking back to the cabin to grab the dog, and if he does..."

His words trailed away, and Denise picked up where he'd left off. "If he does, then I'll welcome him with my gun."

"Good girl," Thompson said, irritating me with the way he addressed his wife. They exchanged a quick I love you before saying goodbye.

Once Thompson was off the other end of the line, Denise finished her search at last, extracting the gun from where it had been hiding.

She picked the semi-automatic up and studied it in her hands. "I was hoping things wouldn't get violent," she said, not realizing the irony of her words.

Not only had they attacked and physically

dragged me here, but they also planned to kill me before the day was through. Not violent, indeed. "

You don't have to do what he says, you know," I whispered quietly, hoping to fill this woman with a sense of sisterhood. "Just because he's the man, that doesn't make him in charge."

"Of course he's in charge," Denise replied with a firm shake of her head. "It's always been that way, but I don't mind."

"All right," I acquiesced.

And then a short while later started in on a different tact. "Tell me about your kids," I suggested.

They had to be around my age. Maybe if I could get her to make that connection, it would warm her to me. Maybe it would save my life.

I'd already decided it was worthless trying to appeal to her husband's sense of humanity. He'd made it clear that when he came back, I'd be taking the long goodbye.

But Denise...

With Denise, I had hope yet.

She rambled on about her two sons and their many, many great accomplishments.

"The boys are both lawyers, like their dad, although they'd both moved out of state after college," Denise explained as her eyelids began to lower.

Yes, this was good. If I could just make her a little sleepier, then maybe I'd have a fighting chance.

"Now that you told me about your sons," I said, keeping my voice at dull and even cadence, "let me tell you about my family. First, there's Nan..." I went into great detail describing every memory I could think of that concerned my grandmother, listing out every single hobby she'd ever expressed even a passing interest in. I hadn't even reached my teen years by the time Denise had nodded off again.

Thank you, Nan. It seemed she was with me in spirit even if she wasn't here physically.

With Denise back asleep, I returned to tugging at my bonds once more. A part of me wished in vain that Denise had left a bit of "painkiller" for me.

As I worked on the rope, I surveyed my surroundings.

Marco dozed happily by the fire. Would waking him up also awaken Denise? Could I convince him to help me even though I didn't have any reason to trust him the way I trusted my own animals?

I just didn't know what to expect from the food-motivated pup, especially since he'd been raised by an owner with exceedingly questionable morals.

That left me to my own devices.

Denise had a gun.

There was also an empty bottle, which could be smashed open and used as a weapon. The dog treats on the mantle may be able to help me control the golden retriever.

And then there were the jagged window shards that still lay scattered along the floor.

Could I lean back far enough in my chair to grab one without tipping over and use that to cut the rope that bound me? Yes, that was my best shot. I just had to take it really slow and hope for the best.

Using the tips of my boots, I pushed my way across the cabin floor, struggling on the carpeted parts, until at last I reached the wall. I used one hand to hold tight to the windowsill, praying it would be enough. If I lost my balance and went crashing to the floor in this chair, that would surely wake Denise—and when she realized what I was doing, I'd be done for.

Maybe she'd even call Thompson who would move up their murderous plans. Not good for me at all. Leaning back, I pushed with my toes and strained with my fingers while leaning back as far as I could. I'd have to let go of the windowsill if I wanted to grab a piece of glass. But would I be able to make it?

First, I had to test everything carefully. Could I take it far enough without toppling over?

Oh, I hoped so.

After what felt like an eternity of maneuvering, testing, and trying, I finally decided to make the grab. I took several deep breaths and forced myself to focus on the task at hand.

This was life and death—and I definitely knew which one I preferred.

I closed my eyes and leaned back toward the floor, only opening them again when I felt the tips of my fingers brush the ground. That was when a heavy figure flew through the window and landed right on my chest, pushing me to the floor amidst the broken shards of glass. Fresh cuts opened on my hands and arms, while the sound of the crash sent Denise jumping to her feet.

What had just attacked me?

Had Thompson come back already?

Was this really the end?

Only one way to find out...

18

Denise screamed, her face turning white with fear. "Get out! Get out of here!" she cried, running to the edge of the cabin and pressing herself flat against the wall.

"Yeesh. What's wrong with her?"

I knew that voice. Pringle!

I watched as he hopped down from my chest and onto the floor below. Oh, I'd never been so happy to see that pesky raccoon in all my life.

"What are you doing here?" I sobbed, tears of relief flowing freely down my cheeks. "How did you know where to find me?"

"Enough with the questions," the raccoon said, tapping his thumb and forefinger together as he thought.

I sat quietly, waiting for him to reveal his master plan, praying desperately that he even had one.

Denise continued to shake and cry, realizing too late that she'd left the gun behind in her desperate need to escape the raccoon.

We both glanced down at the weapon, then our eyes met.

Pringle stood beside me, pushing the shards of glass away with his feet as he slowly cleared a path. He didn't appear to be in much of a hurry.

"Not to pressure you," I said softly, "but I kind of need to know what I'm supposed to do here."

Yes, I was speaking with Pringle right in front of Denise, but right now the only options seemed to be exposing my strange secret or dying an assuredly painful death.

Today, I chose to let my freak flag fly.

"Why are you talking to it?" my captor asked with a ragged shriek. "Get it out of here!"

Pringle drew in a deep breath, his furry shoulders shaking as he attempted to remain calm. "You might want to tell that lady to stop calling me 'it'," he warned. "I ain't no nightmare clown."

I would've laughed, had I not been so terrified. Instead, I simply relayed his message to Denise. "He doesn't like you calling him it. His name is Pringle and he's a boy."

He chittered in annoyance, then corrected me. "I am a man, thank you very much."

"He's a man," I translated, keeping my affect flat.

Denise gawked at the two of us with wide, unblinking eyes. It looked as though she wanted to say something, but only a raspy croak escaped her throat.

"So anyway," the master bandit continued. "Some giant, hairy dog showed up at the house, all panting and excited and saying you'd been carried off. I knew right then and there that it would be up to me to save the day."

I nodded my appreciation and would've hugged him if I hadn't still been tied to my seat.

"He led me back through the woods and now here I am. You miss me?" He smiled, showing off his pointy canines.

"More than you'll ever know," I told him, not caring if I was gushing. I would never punish him for stepping foot in the house again. Not only that, but I would keep him well fed with Fancy Feast, or Delectable Delights, or whatever he wanted. I wasn't above groveling, and I would also make sure to pay my debts, no matter how Pringle wanted them paid.

"I'm so glad you came," I told him. "They're planning to kill me."

"Well, that's a bit extreme," the raccoon observed, then turned toward Denise, taking several quick steps forward.

She pushed herself against the wall, still immobilized from fear.

"Were you really going to kill my neighbor?" he asked, squinting his eyes at her. "That's not very nice!"

Not very nice? Since when had Pringle begun to sound like Paisley? Personally, I had lots of words to describe the Thompsons' plan for me and none of them were anywhere near that mild.

"You think you can untie me?" I couldn't take the chance that Denise would gather her bearings and make a run for the gun. No, I needed to be able to fight for myself when the time came.

And, already, I knew that it would.

"You're really impatient, you know that?" Pringle remarked with a nasally twang as he returned to my side, grabbed one of the larger shards of glass, and began to saw at my binds.

"Don't even give a guy a minute to relax. Do you

know how far I had to run to get here? Ungrateful humans..." He let out a huff of air, and as he continued his work, he chattered along, whether to himself or to me, I wasn't quite sure.

"Anyway, I ran, and I ran. Do you know how deep the snow is out there? And that dog kept talking about pee. Dogs, I tell you. What weird creatures."

Just then, Marco got up from his napping spot by the armchair. I was surprised the ruckus hadn't roused him before.

"Oh, great. Here's another one," Pringle spat. "I'm up to my elbows in canines!"

"Speaking of, where's Cujo?" I asked, feeling one of the threads of twine holding me snap.

"Heck if I know," Pringle answered, continuing his work. "We got close enough for me to smell you for myself. Then the two of us parted ways. He said his job was done, informed me that he's a good boy and that he was going now. But me? I figured I might as well come and see. So what's going on, by the way?"

I swallowed back a sigh. I couldn't appear ungrateful. Not now.

"They kidnapped me and are threatening the mayor so that he'll resign. Then they're going to kill me," I summarized, hating the fact that these words were even coming out of my mouth—let alone that they were true.

"So if the mayor doesn't give in, they're gonna off ya?" Pringle asked, tugging on the rope and then resuming his work with the glass shard.

"Actually they plan to kill me either way."

"Wow. I really do not like this lady. Is it okay if I bite her? Give her a little rabies maybe?"

"Pringle, you do not have rabies," I chastised him. Talk about spreading negative stereotypes. "But yes, you can bite her."

"Lovely," he said, at last delivering the finishing slash to the ropes.

I yanked my hands in front of me and rubbed at my wrists where they'd gone raw.

Free! This felt so good.

Now I just had to... Oh no.

Denise had finally begun to move again, and she was rushing right to the gun. I moved as quick as I could, throwing myself halfway across the room, but I already knew I'd lost.

19

I didn't reach the gun first, but neither did Denise.

Pringle stood on the side table, clutching the gun to his chest as if it were a precious child. Given his size, the simple handgun looked more like a powerful rifle.

"Wheee, look at me! I'm the terminator!" He flipped the semi-automatic around and pointed it toward the fireplace. "I'll be back, baby! Hasta la pasta!"

My heart thudded behind my ribcage. I didn't want Denise to have a gun, but it was every bit as dangerous in Pringle's paws. "Put the gun down," I pleaded, too afraid to ask him to hand it to me directly.

"What do you mean *put it down?* I just got it! This is awesome! Seriously, how cool do I look right now?" He squinted one eye shut and brought his furry fingers to the trigger and—

The bullet flew right for the stone fireplace, tore through the flames, and then ricocheted back into the cabin.

"Duck!" I shouted, throwing myself to the floor as the bullet shattered another of the windows and disappeared into the snowy wilderness outside.

Denise gasped for air loudly and repeatedly. If I hadn't heard the bullet exit through the window, I'd have worried she'd been hit. Instead, she seemed to be having a panic attack.

Unlike my captor, I'd been in dangerous scrapes plenty of times before—never with an armed rodent, but still.

I pushed myself to my feet, ignoring the pain in my hands and wrists.

Pringle was staring down the barrel of his gun as if a peek inside would explain how the firing mechanism had just been triggered. If I tried to take it from him, it would probably go off again. I had to talk us out of this one, but first there was something else I needed.

In the rush for the handgun, Denise had

forgotten her other asset—a working cell phone. I yanked it off the table and punched in a call to emergency services.

"What are you doing?" Denise cried. "No!"

"What's your emergency?" the operator on the other end of the line asked, but before I could answer, the gun fired a second time.

Denise screamed, and I spun myself around, expecting to find a dead woman, a dead raccoon, or both.

What I found truly surprised me. The golden retriever had pounced on Pringle, knocking the gun from the raccoon's furry, little hands. "Guns are for hunting. Not for hurting," he warned with a growl that bared his teeth.

I'd never seen a retriever look quite so menacing. Apparently it took a lot to send him into attack dog mode—or more precisely a rogue raccoon with a gun.

Marco snarled, the long sandy hair on his back rising at the hackles.

Denise continued to hyperventilate and cry.

Pringle chittered from his place beneath the much larger dog's paws. "You're not going to kill me. Are you? Look, I'm one of the good guys. You can tell by my charming smile. See." He raised his gums and showed his teeth, which the dog took as a threat.

Marco reared back, then lunged for Pringle's throat. *No!*

CRASH!

Another furry figure crashed through the window. This time it was Cujo, and he did not look happy.

"So it was your pee I smelled," he told the golden. "I should have known you were a no-good useless—"

"Quiet!" Marco snapped. "I'm the first dog of Glendale, and I will not be talked to that way!"

"Unhand that raccoon. He's not a villain. He's a hero!"

"Then why does he have a gun?"

"It's true. He was saving me! She's the one who was going to kill me!" I pointed at Denise, who sat rocking in the corner looking completely unthreatening.

"Her?" Marco whined. "But she gave me treats. Two treats! How can she be bad?"

"Oh, my fellow dog, you have much to learn about humans and their motives," Cujo said with a shake of his head. "Come. Let's share a pee outside, and I'll fill you in."

The dogs turned to leave, and I made a beeline for the gun. Yes, this time I reached it first. Mostly because no one else had attempted to collect it.

Pringle lay on the floor, too shocked to move. From what I could tell, Marco hadn't hurt him yet. Still, Pringle had never been outmaneuvered before. His pride was now hurt more than anything else.

I emptied the magazine, dropping the remaining bullets to the floor so no more dangerous mishaps could happen.

"Can I have that back?" Pringle asked, slowly bringing himself to a seated position.

"I'll buy you a Nerf gun when we get home. Much safer, and then you can use the soft ammo to play target practice with Octo-Cat." My cat was going to kill me, but at least the Thompsons hadn't managed to yet.

I ambled toward the door and opened it wide in case the dogs decided to come back inside. No need to force them through the broken glass when there was a perfectly good door on hand.

Although I'd complained about the bitter cold that same morning, now I sucked in the fresh air with a happy sigh. It felt good to be alive.

But we weren't out of the woods yet. Mr. Thompson could still come back at any time, and...

Speaking of woods, three people ran out from them and into the open field, Nan among them.

I ran outside, crying with relief.

When I flung my arms around her, Paisley yipped, "Mommy! I'm here, too!"

I laughed when I noticed her in the carrier on Nan's chest and gave her a nice scratch between those giant ears of hers.

The other two people were Officer Bouchard and one of the newer cops I didn't yet know by name.

Bouchard came over and placed a heavy hand on my shoulder. "We heard shots fired. Are you okay?"

I nodded so vigorously, my hair fell into my face. "Yes. Yes. I'm okay. But..." I let my words fall away as I motioned toward the cabin.

Both policemen drew their guns and headed inside.

Nan was quick to follow, dragging me along.

We were slowed by my injuries, but arrived just moments after the officers. Already, they had Denise Thompson in handcuffs and were pulling her onto her feet.

"Are you the one who took my granddaughter?" Nan asked, marching straight up to her.

"Yes, but I—"

Nan came in close, readying a punch, but before she could make contact, Denise cried out in pain.

"Ouch! It hurts so bad!"

Nan turned to me in confusion, which is when I noticed Paisley, a bit of blood lining her muzzle.

"That little rat bit me in the boob!" Denise screamed, motioning toward Paisley with her chin.

Nan and I turned toward one another and broke out laughing. "Good dog!" we both cried in unison.

"Yay, I helped!" Paisley sang as the officers escorted Denise away from the scene.

20

The doorbell rang, and I rushed to open it. My boyfriend, Charles, stood waiting on the other side.

"I keep telling you to just let yourself in," I teased him, looping my arms around his neck and accepting a kiss.

"No more almost dying at the hands of former partners at my law firm," he chastised me.

I stuck out my tongue playfully. "Fine, I'll stay away from the partners and stick to associates."

"Not funny."

Hmm, I thought it was.

The great cabin affair had started and finished just two days ago. Both Thompsons were in jail awaiting their bail hearing, while Mark Dennison had been forced to resign despite his best laid plans.

Me? I'd slept for a solid twenty-four hours straight despite Octo-Cat's constant mewling outside my door. That guy had no patience. I'd almost died, and yet that wasn't a good enough excuse for him.

That brought us to today. Nan and I had invited Charles and my parents over for a special celebratory feast, and—boy—did we have a lot to celebrate.

Not only had I solved what would have been my first paying case, if the client hadn't been arrested as a result of my investigation, but we also had a roomwarming for Octo-Cat and a hero's party for Pringle.

The tabby had claimed the room beside my library. Due to my "lengthy frolic through the woods" as he liked to call my near-death encounter, he'd had plenty of time to plan the decorations, based on a combination of old sitcoms he liked and a mobile game called Matchington Mansion.

"Make sure my three pillows don't match," he'd warned seriously. "Otherwise, they'll disappear, and we don't want that happening."

Even though I questioned his grip on reality, I did as he instructed, even though installing a one-hundred- and forty-gallon tropical fish tank in the upstairs bedroom had proven both exhausting and expensive.

It was now his prized possession, though, and he spent long-hours fantasizing about devouring his scaly new pets. He was definitely lucky that I was a better pet owner than him.

"Are we all here?" Nan asked, emerging from the kitchen in her favorite apron.

The doorbell rang again, and my parents pushed their way inside. As soon as she saw me, my mom grabbed my head and peppered kisses all over my face.

"Oh, my baby!" she exclaimed.

"I'm not a baby," I grumbled in a futile attempt to extricate myself from her embrace.

"Ahh, but you'll always be our baby," Dad said with a chuckle.

Charles placed a protective arm around me, knowing I'd blow a gasket if my parents didn't cool it on the smothering and give me some space.

"To the table!" my grandmother shouted. She'd already laid out our best china, insisting that she preferred I rest rather than try to help.

Now she scuttled into the kitchen and returned

with a tray of personal-sized potpies. My mouth watered in anticipation.

"No one takes a bite until our guest of honor arrives," she warned, shaking a finger at my father.

"Say no more, I have arrived," Octo-Cat declared, hopping onto the table beside me.

"She means Pringle," I whispered. Everyone here knew my secret, but it still felt a bit odd to converse so openly with the animals.

"Pringle? What's so special about that guy?"

"Um, he saved my life," I answered with a shrug.

My cat snorted and licked at the pie on my plate.

"Gross!" I cried.

"Don't worry, I've made pies for him and Paisley, too. We'll just swap yours for his. But it means he'll be getting the chicken, and you'll have the shrimp."

"Ha!" I cried in delight. Personally, I'd probably rather have the chicken, but knowing that Octo-Cat's bad attitude had cost him his favorite food gave me endless joy.

The electronic pet door zinged in the other room, and in walked Pringle, wearing his new chipped collar. Now he could come and go whenever he pleased; no invite required.

I knew I'd regret that soon enough, but—hey—I owed him my life.

Everyone cheered and clapped while the critter basked in the attention.

"This is all great. Very great," he informed me. "But can they maybe sing a song of my greatness?"

"Like 'For he's a jolly good fellow'?" I suggested.

He considered this for a moment. "That will do for now, but I'd really prefer a custom ballad."

We all sang as instructed, then enjoyed Nan's delicious meal. When we'd finished, I rushed to the coat closet and pulled out a present I'd wrapped carefully in custom wrapping paper pattered with the Pringles chips logo.

"Awww, you shouldn't have!" the raccoon guest of honor exclaimed. "But I'm so very glad you did!"

He tore through the wrapping paper in short order, then bit into the box, and...

"My very own gun! Yes!" he cried.

"Not so fast," I exclaimed. "Do you remember what we talked about?"

He cast his eyes down in shame. "Guns are dangerous, and I'm not the terminator."

"Yes, and?"

"And?"

"Read the label on the box. This is a Nerf gun. Do you remember what I told you about Nerf guns?"

A smile crept across his face as realization dawned in his beady black eyes. "Roger that," he said, loading a foam dart into the gun with far more skill than he'd handled the semi-automatic at the cabin.

Biting his tongue and squinting one eye, he aimed and—

"Ahh! I am wounded!" Octo-Cat cried as he fell from his spot on the table.

I gave Pringle a high five. I couldn't wait to tell Cujo about this when I saw him on our next run.

Although it hadn't quite gone as planned, I'd never forget our first paying case. Not in a million years.

Is Octo-Cat a new daddy? You've gotta be kitten me!

CLICK HERE to get your copy of *Lawless Litter*, so that you can keep reading this series today!

* * *

And make sure you're on Molly's list so that you hear about all the new releases, monthly giveaways, and other cool stuff (including lots and lots of cat pics).

You can do that here:
MollyMysteries.com/subscribe

WHAT'S NEXT?

It's kittens for Octo-Cat when an orphaned litter shows up at our doorstep. And although the needy litter may be cute, the deadly mystery they bring with them is anything but.

Charles has been hinting at a big surprise he's planned for our first Valentine's Day together, but the arrival of the kittens quickly changes everything. Now he's helping me figure out who put the babies on my porch and why their paws are covered in blood.

Meanwhile Octo-Cat is left to play babysitter to the unruly brood while we investigate, and he's none too happy about it.

Right, so all we have to do is keep the kittens safe, solve their mystery, find forever homes for them, and try to find a way to salvage Valentine's Day. That shouldn't be too impossible...

LAWLESS LITTER is now available.

CLICK HERE to get your copy so that you can keep reading this series today!

Hi, my name's Angie Russo. I used to be a paralegal, but now I'm a full-time private investigator... well, at least in theory.

We only get about one case per month, and they only sometimes pay. Luckily, my cat came with a very generous trust fund from his previous owner, which solves at least one major problem.

Oh, also, my cat talks.

Not to everyone, though.

Just me.

Considering his constant stream of criticism and unwanted life advice, I'm sure he wouldn't have the time to talk to anyone else even if he were able.

Did I mention he's my partner?

No, not like that. He's my *business* partner.

My romantic partner is a handsome, brainy, sweet, and considerate attorney by the name of Charles Longfellow, III. And while I may call him "sweetie," my cat calls him "UpChuck."

I'll probably have to cave soon and make a deal with Mr. Kitty to get him to stop that. Valentine's Day is just around the corner, and I don't want anything to ruin it for us.

Besides, Octo-Cat should be busy with his own date that night. He and his long-distance girlfriend, former show cat Grizabella, are as in love as any two cats could be. I should know, because he's constantly lording it over in front of me, saying how much better his relationship is than mine.

Cats, am I right?

Well, I also have a dog—a little rescue Chihuahua named Paisley. She technically belongs to my nan, but we all live together.

Paisley is sweet like a double scoop of double fudge ice cream covered in sprinkles and chocolate sauce. Sometimes she's too optimistic about people's intentions, which means she's not exactly the best crime-solving partner.

Nan, on the other hand, uses all her varied life

experience to solve our cases in the most unusual way possible. As a former Broadway actress, she's all about costumes, accents, and general over-the-topness.

Boy, do I love her for it.

Speaking of love, I have a bit of a love-hate relationship with the raccoon who lives in my back yard. His name is Pringle and he has zero boundaries. Not too long ago, he uncovered a long-buried family secret by snooping around the attic—we still haven't fully resolved that one—but he also kind of saved my life a couple weeks ago. I guess that makes us even.

As a thank-you, I now allow him to come into the house whenever he pleases. And he "pleases" quite often. Our grocery bill has risen precipitously. Meanwhile, Pringle is beginning to resemble a literal fuzz ball with all the junk food he puts away on a daily basis.

Sometimes I wish I'd never had that near-death experience that left me with my ability to talk to animals, but then I remember all the amazing things I've gained in life since then. Don't tell him, but the greatest of those things is my friendship with Octo-Cat.

Sure, he only sometimes shows me affection,

but when he does it's enough to keep a smile on my face all day.

That brings us to today.

It's been T-minus six days since my cat deigned to let me pet him. My parents have been on a glamorous Alaskan cruise for the past three days, and I have had no cases since investigating the mayor's missing golden retriever last month.

All this downtime has got me wondering whether I should take up a hobby while I wait for the next big case to land in my lap. I have tried advertising, but that's mostly been a bust. So what else can I really do?

Ugh.

Maybe I should go back to school and finally work toward a bachelor's degree in Criminal Justice or something.

I have seven associate degrees, because I've always loved learning too much to commit to any one field for four whole years. But now that I'm a PI, I can't picture any other life for me. Would a degree help bolster the confidence of potential clients?

Or maybe someday I could officially join the police force and work as a salaried detective? Would they let me forgo a human partner in favor of my cat?

Hmm. If not, that might be a deal-breaker.

So many options, but none of them are just right.

I'm pretty sure I know what I need to do, and it's the one thing I've been trying so desperately to avoid ever since I got started.

My boyfriend Charles is the senior partner at his law firm and has offered on more than one occasion to hire me through the firm to help with cases. Sure, Charles was a good boss while I worked for him as a paralegal—in fact, that's how we first met and became friends.

But our relationship has evolved so much since then, and I'm worried it might hurt the good thing we have going together. Also, returning to the law firm feels like a giant step back even if my job title would change.

I guess what I'm trying to tell you is that I just don't know what to do.

Maybe the cat would be willing to decide for me...

* * *

O cto-Cat regarded me with a piteous look. He flicked his tail and knocked a bottle of painkillers from the nightstand on which he was perched. "See, this right here. *This* is why you need me."

I'd planned to do a little reading before tucking in for the night, but the two of us had gotten to talking about my conundrum and—as expected—the tabby had no shortage of opinions.

"Think about it," he continued, swinging the tip of his tail like a metronome. "Everything you have is because of me. House. Job. Boyfriend. Need I go on?"

I swallowed down my comeback. Sad to say, he was right. I hated that he was right.

"So what should I do?" I asked with wide eyes.

"Isn't it obvious?" He narrowed his eyes at me, then groaned. "Oh, right. Forgot who I was talking to for a moment there."

I resisted the urge to pick him up and carry him out into the hall so that I could shut the door between us and finally get some peace.

Octo-Cat, however, continued his lecture unaware of just how painfully it was being received. "You should take the work from UpChuck. *Duh.*"

"Don't call him that," I mumbled.

He rolled his large amber eyes. "You need more experience and references, and he's offering to help you get those. It's not just *you* you have to think about here."

I bit my thumbnail and sighed. "Okay," I said simply. "I'll talk to him tomorrow then."

My tabby seemed pleased with this conclusion. "Now are there any other parts of your life that you need me to fix for you tonight, or can I go about my nightly duties?"

"What nightly duties?" This was the first I'd heard of them, and while Octo-Cat *did* help solve cases, he did precious little else with his days. Could the nights really be all that different?

"Oh, you know. Keeping my favorite spot on the couch warm. Walking over all the counters and tables to make sure they're still sturdy. Protecting the house from ghosts. Watching the—"

"Wait. Go back a second there. Ghosts?"

He glared at me as if I should have known better than to interrupt his soliloquy. "Yes. Didn't you know? Only cats can see them."

I studied him for a second in an attempt to figure out whether he was being serious, but he just stared at me blankly, giving absolutely nothing away.

"Are ghosts really *real?*" I squeaked. I knew I had something of a magical ability, but I had a hard time believing that those fairytale supernatural creatures walked among us.

My cat yawned, and his smelly tuna breath hit me full-on in the face. "Guess you'll never know," he said flippantly before jumping off the side table and trotting out of the room.

Ghosts? *Huh.*

Something told me I might not sleep so well that night.

What happens next?
Don't wait to find out...

Read the next two chapters right now in Molly Fitz's free book app.

Or purchase your copy so that you can keep reading this zany mystery series today!

MORE MOLLY

ABOUT MOLLY FITZ

While USA Today bestselling author Molly Fitz can't technically talk to animals, she and her doggie best friend, Sky Princess, have deep and very animated conversations as they navigate their days. Add to that, five more dogs, a snarky feline, comedian husband, and diva daughter, and you can pretty much imagine how life looks at the Casa de Fitz.

Molly lives in a house on a high hill in the Michigan woods and occasionally ventures out for good food, great coffee, or to meet new animal friends.

Writing her quirky, cozy animal mysteries is

pretty much a dream come true, but sometimes she also goes by the names Melissa Storm and Mila Riggs and writes a very different kind of story.

Learn more, grab the free app, or sign up for her newsletter at **www.MollyMysteries.com**!

PET WHISPERER P.I.

Angie Russo just partnered up with Blueberry Bay's first ever talking cat detective. Along with his ragtag gang of human and animal helpers, Octo-Cat is determined to save the day... so long as it doesn't interfere with his schedule. Start with book 1, ***Kitty Confidential***.

PARANORMAL TEMP AGENCY

Tawny Bigford's simple life takes a turn for the magical when she stumbles upon her landlady's murder and is recruited by a talking black cat named Fluffikins to take over the deceased's role as the official Town Witch for Beech Grove, Georgia. Start with book 1, **Witch for Hire**.

MERLIN THE MAGICAL FLUFF

Gracie Springs is not a witch... but her cat is. Now she must help to keep his secret or risk spending the rest of her life in some magical prison. Too bad trouble seems to find them at every turn! Start with book 1, **Merlin the Magical Fluff**.

THE MEOWING MEDIUM

Mags McAllister lives a simple life making candles for tourists in historic Larkhaven, Georgia. But when a cat with mismatched eyes enters her life, she finds herself with the ability to see into the realm of spirits... Now the ghosts of people long dead have started coming to her for help solving their cold cases. Start with book 1, **Secrets of the Specter**.

THE PAINT-SLINGING SLEUTH

Following a freak electrical storm, Lisa Lewis's vibrant paintings of fairytale creatures have started coming to life. Unfortunately, only she can see and communicate with them. And when her mentor turns up dead, this aspiring artist must turn amateur sleuth to clear her name and save the day with only these "pigments" of her imagination to help her. Start with book 1, **My Colorful Conundrum**.

SPECIAL COLLECTIONS

Black Cat Crossing
Pet Whisperer P.I. Books 1-3
Pet Whisperer P.I. Books 4-6
Pet Whisperer P.I. Books 7-9
Pet Whisperer P.I. Books 10-12

CONNECT WITH MOLLY

Sign up for my newsletter and get a special digital prize pack for joining, including an exclusive story, Meowy Christmas Mayhem, fun quiz, and lots of cat pictures!

mollymysteries.com/subscribe

Have you ever wanted to talk to animals? You can chat with Octo-Cat and help him solve an exclusive online mystery here:

mollymysteries.com/chat

Or maybe you'd like to chat with other animal-loving readers as well as to learn about new books and giveaways as soon as they happen! Come join Molly's VIP reader group on Facebook.

mollymysteries.com/group

MORE BOOKS LIKE THIS

Welcome to Whiskered Mysteries, where each and every one of our charming cozies comes with a furry sidekick... or several! Around here, you'll find we're all about crafting the ultimate reading experience. Whether that means laugh-out-loud antics, jaw-dropping magical exploits, or whimsical journeys through small seaside towns, you decide.

So go on and settle into your favorite comfy chair and grab one of our *paw*some cozy mysteries to kick off your next great reading adventure!

Visit our website to browse our books and meet our authors, to jump into our discussion group, or to join our newsletter. See you there!

www.WhiskeredMysteries.com

Made in the USA
Las Vegas, NV
24 April 2023

71022646R00118